PRAISE FOR

Lammie Loves Cubby

" In a town that time forgot, Lammie Timmons secretly waits for Cubby Tatum. She's loved him since kindergarten. Living with Mama and working for Attorney Morton is a small price to pay for love delayed. And after twenty years he's finally back. Cubby Tatem is fire and Lammie is air. Together, their flames reach the heavens, leaving trails of ash for arson investigator Maureen Boykin to prod and pry. *Lammie Loves Cubby* will attract readers like moths to flame. Nora Gaskin is back with her best book yet: the tale of two singed souls who'd have been better off never reuniting."

— **Sara E. Johnson**, author of the Alexa Glock Forensic Mysteries

" Sparks fly in this small-town drama where lovely kleptomaniac—Lammie—and handsome pyromaniac—Cubby—fall so deeply in love that their passion to protect each and their bad habits lead them to a fiery and uncertain future. When a determined fire investigator and a do-gooder who lives in a van team up to figure out why the community is on fire, the couple's dream of a happily-ever-after is in jeopardy. And when the lovebirds don't realize that revenge is a dish best served cold, the heat is on. *Lammie Loves Cubby* is a quick read that will leave you wondering: is it possible to put out a flame and keep it burning too?"

— **Landis Wade**, award-winning author of *Deadly Declarations* and founder of Charlotte Readers Podcast

" *Our Town* meets *Bonnie and Clyde* in Nora Gaskin's *Lammie Loves Cubby*. The motto of Littleboro, NC, where the story is set, may be "The Little Town Time Forgot," but readers won't soon forget the wacky antics of Gaskin's characters in this fast-paced and fun novel."

—**Heather Newton**, author of *The Puppeteer's Daughters*

" The power of love, the power of fire. One gives rise to the other. Throw in secrets and you've got a dynamic story about how flawed characters deal with each other—and life. In fact, the beauty of this novel is that it looks at these characters' contradictions with such bracing honesty that it gives us hope for them. I highly recommend *Lammie Loves Cubby*. It's a clear-eyed, quirky, compelling book."

—**Judy Goldman**, author of *The Rest of Our Lives*

LAMMIE LOVES CUBBY

NORA GASKIN

LYSTRA BOOKS
& Literary Services

Lammie Loves Cubby
Copyright © 2026 by Nora Gaskin Esthimer.
All rights reserved.

ISBN 979-8-9921363-9-5 paperback
ISBN 979-8-9935520-0-2 ebook
Library of Congress Control Number 2025927376

The contents of this book are the intellectual property of Nora Gaskin Esthimer. Except for brief excerpts for reviews, no portion of the text may be reproduced in any form without written permission from the author or publisher. Contact the publisher at the address below.

Book design by Kelly Prelipp Lojk.

Author photo by Nancy Chescheir.

LYSTRA BOOKS
& Literary Services

Published by Lystra Books & Literary Services, LLC
391 Lystra Estates Drive
Chapel Hill, NC 27517
lystrabooks@gmail.com

For Steve, Again and Always

ALSO BY NORA GASKIN

Until Proven: A Mystery in Two Parts
A NOVEL

Time of Death
NONFICTION

The Worst Thing
A NOVEL

Available through bookstores
and online book sellers.

March and April 1976

1

Lammie Timmons got the best news, news she'd waited more than twenty years for, at quarter past nine on a Monday morning.

Up until then, it had been like any Monday, or any other day. Lammie had walked three blocks from home to the office on Courthouse Square. On the way, she saw Miss Leora Mack across the street, already pulling the early spring weeds in her rose bed and keeping an eye on things. Miss Leora called, "hoo hoo." Lammie looked away.

Neighbors walking their dogs or driving past waved at Lammie. She flicked her wrist to respond. She nodded to acquaintances on Court Street and kept going.

She stopped into the post office to collect Saturday's business mail and allowed the post master to tell her the sight of her pretty face bright and early every Monday made life worth living, then walked along the square to the building where she worked, took the elevator to the third floor, unlocked the office door, hung up her coat, put her purse in the bottom drawer of her desk, and started the coffee.

The weekend cleaning man always left her brass nameplate askew. She wiped his fingerprints off and straightened it. Mary Lambert Timmons. She flipped the desk calendar page to the new day, week, and month just before Attorney Morton opened the office door, stepped in, and stopped. He didn't say his usual, "Morning, Lammie. What's on our docket for today?"

Instead, he put his right hand on his heart. "I've got the worst news, Lammie. Mr. Bear Tatum is very ill, won't live much longer."

Heat rose up Lammie's neck, and she looked down so he couldn't see her face turn pink. She pressed her lips tight to hold back a smile. She had waited all these years for Bear Tatum's son Cubby to come home. Surely he would now that his father was dying.

Her gaze rested on the desk calendar's fresh page, March 1, 1976. A day she would never forget.

Attorney Morton was not a tall man, but he carried himself with assurance of his own importance, and he was a talker. Lammie had questions, but she knew all she had to do was wait, and she'd get them answered without having to ask.

Attorney Morton sighed as he crossed the reception area and set a white paper sack on her desk. The sack held a fresh, still-warm cinnamon bun for her and a sausage and egg biscuit for himself. His wife didn't allow him to eat sausage, or eggs, or biscuits, and she believed Lammie kept him in check at the office. The cinnamon bun every Monday was a bribe.

"Yes." He sighed again. "Miss Dru, Bear's sister—you know she moved in to keep house for him after his wife died—she called me after church yesterday, asked me to come out to see him."

He went on and on—Mr. Bear was still good in his mind, knew what was going on, wanted to be sure he had all his affairs in order. "It is a shame to see a big, strapping man like Bear laid low."

That made Attorney Morton recall going to Littleboro High School football games when he was just a boy. Bear—so nicknamed because he was a husky baby who became a husky man—was the star fullback. All-State. The last time Littleboro had a state championship team.

"What's that poem? 'Look on my works, ye mighty'? Something like that." Attorney Morton sighed yet again.

Lammie knew everything he could possibly tell her about the Tatums. She gleaned, gathered, treasured news of the Tatums. Any mention of them in the local paper, any bits of information she overheard, any sighting of Mr. Bear around Courthouse Square, where his insurance business occupied a building, any news he let drop when he met with Attorney Morton—Lammie filed it all away in her memory.

"Your biscuit's getting cold," she said. "I'll bring your coffee." She stood and had to rest her hands on the desktop for a moment, knees weak from the news.

"Get the Tatum file too. I told Bear everything is in perfect order, but maybe I should take a quick look-see while he's still with us." He went into his office, shaking his head, carrying the biscuit wrapped in waxed paper and a napkin.

Lammie pulled the file, got her boss's coffee, and carried both to his office.

"Is Miss Dru alone with him?" She couldn't resist one question that would lead to more information.

"They have nursing help. And Bear's son is on his way. Been in the army since he graduated high school. Maybe you know that. Ran track, as I recall. Never was the athlete his father was. But I guess he's done all right in the service. More than twenty years now."

Did Lammie know Cubby Tatum was in the army? She'd been in love with him since she was five years old. She knew.

She watched Attorney Morton unwrap the biscuit and all but pray over it. She waited and was rewarded.

"Miss Dru says Bear will hold on till his son gets here. The boy was planning to retire anyway, it seems. This just sped things up. He's got to get the army's red tape dealt with, and he'll be home."

Attorney Morton took a sip of coffee and pinched a browned edge off the top half of his biscuit.

Lammie slipped out of the room and went back to her chair.

She studied the date on her calendar again. Cubby Tatum was coming home.

Lammie had loved Cubby since they were in kindergarten at the Little Red School House. They were alphabetical, Tatum and Timmons. They held hands when the children lined up two-by-two and walked to the drug store for lemonade or to the town auditorium for the Christmas pageant. Some boys didn't want to hold hands with girls or each other, but Cubby reached for hers every time and didn't let go until they got to where they were going.

Because her daddy died in August, she started first grade in a different school and came back to Littleboro Elementary after Christmas vacation. Mama took Lammie to the principal's office and left her there because Mama had to work for a living now and didn't have time to spend waiting.

The first-grade teacher, Miss Fitzgerald, came and walked Lammie down the hall, into a classroom, and to the table she'd share with another student. It was Cubby. They were still alphabetical.

"Hello, Lammie." He looked at her and smiled, as if he'd been waiting for her.

"Hello, Cubby," she said.

By third grade, the children lined up single file and no longer held hands, so now Lammie saw the back of Cubby's head. She discovered the constellation of freckles on the back of his neck. She walked behind him all the rest of the elementary grades and studied those freckles. They rose and fell under shorter or longer hair, under collars and jackets. If they disappeared, she knew not to worry. They'd be back.

In junior high and high school, Lammie and Cubby were often in the same classes, and she sat behind him again. He smiled when she passed by, turned around to ask if she had an extra pencil. When he bent his head over his book, she could see the freckles. Always there.

The night they processed down the aisle of the town auditorium to receive their high school diplomas, she was right behind him. Cubby had a fresh haircut, his neck shaved. The freckles were bright and shimmered a little through the tears that welled in her eyes.

It wasn't the solemnity of the commencement ceremony that made Lammie want to cry. The whispered news had gone around during rehearsal—Cubby, whom everyone expected to go to Carolina, come home, and join his daddy's business—had enlisted in the army. He would soon be gone without knowing she loved him. She would have told him if she'd known earlier, would have found the courage somehow.

Lammie knew that every year a bunch of kids from Littleboro went to Myrtle Beach after graduation. Cubby would be among them—the crowd she'd never been part of, who got a little wild and wound up skinny-dipping at dawn.

She could imagine it all, could imagine Cubby's bare bottom and flat stomach. Her own stomach flipped. She stared at the freckles and almost stepped on his heels when they got up on the stage and waited to hear their names called. She could have said it then. Whispered it to him.

"Bernard Quinn Tatum Jr.," the principal called, so the school superintendent could hand Cubby his diploma, then "Mary Lambert Timmons."

She followed Cubby for the last time.

Lammie went home with her mother and Aunt Serena who had come to town specially for the night. No wildness. No beach. No Cubby.

Mama and Aunt Serena drank the bottle of cold duck they'd bought for celebration, minus the one small glass they poured for Lammie, and then went on to drink bourbon on the screened back porch and laugh and squabble while Lammie went to her bedroom and wept for Cubby.

Somehow over the twenty years and more since then, she had come to believe—no, to know—that she would see him again, that love delayed was not love denied. Knowing that, she could go on.

And now it would happen.

That Monday, March 1, 1976—the good news day—Lammie got home at five thirty. Mama greeted her at the front door. "Did you hear about Bear Tatum?"

"I heard. From Attorney Morton. How did you know?" Lammie hung her coat in the closet under the stairs.

"It's all over town." Mama had a tall glass with a lot of ice and what might have been tea. Or bourbon and water. Lammie walked down the short hallway to the kitchen. Yes, the bottle was out. Mama followed her.

"Are you cooking tonight, Mama? Want me to?"

"I plan to. A meatloaf maybe. Then we'll have leftovers."

There were no signs of meatloaf being underway. It'd be nine o'clock before they ate, if she left it to Mama. If they ate at all.

"I'll make us some hamburger steaks and mashed potatoes," Lammie said.

"Whatever you want." Mama waved her hand, not the one with the glass in it.

"Just let me change clothes."

"Mr. Bear was so good to us when your daddy died. So kind. Remember?" Mama trailed Lammie back down the hall.

"You always say that. And I always say, I was too young to remember."

It wasn't only because she had been six years old that Lammie didn't remember. Mama sent Lammie to stay with Daddy's parents on their farm right after the funeral. Lammie had cried at being made to go, but Granny and Granddaddy loved her so much, she cried harder at Christmas time when Mama came to get her.

Lammie did remember that Mr. Bear always greeted her with friendly concern anytime she saw him around town, or he came to see Attorney Morton. "Lammie, how are you? Your daddy would be so proud." And so forth, so on. To her, Bear Tatum was good for one thing. Cubby.

Lammie went upstairs to her room and closed the door. She wanted to linger where she felt safest and think about Cubby, but she needed to get some food into Mama. Bedtime would come soon enough, and that was her time for thinking and planning. She changed into a pair of gray corduroy pants and a navy blue sweater, took a deep breath, headed downstairs.

2

Bear Tatum lingered a week, then passed quietly at home with his son and sister by his side. The funeral was to be Thursday, March 11, at his childhood home church west of town, Silver Creek Presbyterian.

"Let's get there early," Lammie told Mama. "We don't want to have to park on the road and walk."

"I'll be ready before you are."

That would be a first.

Lammie studied her closet. The little church was old, plain, drafty, but she'd been there when it was packed full, and if the furnace was chugging away, as was likely, people would be dabbing sweat. She put on a black dress in lightweight wool, lined so she didn't need a slip. It had a scoop neck—the sales lady said it showed off her nice collar bones—and cap sleeves. She could wear her black bouclé jacket and take it off when the place got too hot. Kitten heels. The pearl necklace and earrings she'd bought for herself.

Lipstick. She wanted the red but settled for a sedate pink.

"Mama," she called as she left her room. "Ten minutes."

But Mama was already at the foot of the stairs. She frowned when she saw Lammie. "Oh, honey, that black's too harsh for your coloring. Why don't you put on your dove gray suit? You're hardly Victoria mourning Albert."

"I'll go start the car."

The little church's parking lot was almost empty. Two funeral home cars stood at the front door, but no one was in sight.

Lammie parked under a big oak tree. A blue car pulled in beside them.

"That's Helen and Freda," Mama said. She got out and greeted her friends.

Lammie turned the rearview mirror and checked her lips to buy a little time. When she joined the three ladies, Helen and Freda exclaimed over the dress and jacket. "You put us all to shame, Lammie. Always the best dressed."

A back-handed complement. They'd be thinking what Mama had said, too harsh for her complexion, but they were not who Lammie cared about.

Two more cars, then two more, turned into the church yard.

"We're going to get the best seats." Mama hurried them all to the door and inside.

Mama said, "Down front, please," to an usher, and the four of them followed the man down the aisle. The pianist played a soft rendition of "In the Garden." The gleaming mahogany casket sat on a stand draped in royal blue. The sight sobered them, drew them forward.

The usher showed them to the first pew behind those reserved for family and gave them each a program. Heavy cream paper, deckled edges, a photo of Bear Tatum in his prime.

Lammie made sure to get the aisle seat, even though the man tried to move her to the middle. She'd let somebody crawl over her before she'd give up a chance to see Cubby up close when he passed by. Mama sat beside her, then Freda and Helen.

A wreath of white carnations and roses with a black banner, "Gone but Not Forgotten," stood in front of the casket. Smaller arrangements were set up around it, filling the space. Lilies, mums, glads. All white. A bit much for the little country church.

"Closed casket," Helen murmured.

"He was so wasted at the end." Mama and the ladies tutted and sighed.

Lammie remembered, Daddy's casket had been closed. How did Mama explain it for a young man who wasn't wasted? Not until years later when Lammie found the Littleboro Gazette's back issues on microfiche at the library did she understand why.

She glanced at Mama. Her face was composed, her eyes on the program. Was she thinking about Daddy, too, or just Mr. Bear Tatum? Or anything at all?

Behind them, people came in, filling the rows, feet shuffling, throats clearing, layers of hushed voices piling up, filling the space. Funny how loud quiet could be. The piano player changed over to "Little Brown Church in the Vale."

Lammie shrugged out of her bouclé jacket and folded it on her lap. Under the cover of the music, the three ladies beside her kept up their commentary.

Helen: "When did the son get here?"

Mama: "Saturday night about midnight, I heard. In time to say goodbye."

It was Lammie who'd had that news first, again from Attorney Morton. She regretted telling Mama, giving her the gift of knowing something Helen didn't.

Freda: "Calla lilies give me the creeps."

Mama always complained that Freda complained too much, nitpicked. Lammie agreed with Freda.

Helen: "I sent those lilies."

Lammie looked at her watch. Ten till eleven. Would Mama, Helen, and Freda zig and zag the whole time?

Freda: "I took them a chicken casserole."

Yes, they would. Lammie looked at her watch again. Eight till eleven. Cubby would have arrived by now. They were under the same roof again.

Helen: "I took my yeast rolls."

Mama: "My succotash."

Would the family be escorted in early or at eleven on the dot? Or would they be late?

Freda: "Mary Ruth, not succotash."

Mama: "What's wrong with succotash?"

Lammie's mind rose, floated to the ceiling, became a mist. Something she had a lot of practice doing. Every day of her life. It was that or go crazy.

Freda: "I can't stand lima beans."

Mama: "Well, I finish it with a dash of cream so you wouldn't even know."

Freda: "Oh, I'd know."

Helen: "Do you suppose Bear provided for Dru in his will? Wouldn't you hate to be beholden to a nephew?"

The nephew was Cubby. Lammie's mind settled into her body again. She dug her fingers into the nubbly jacket fabric.

The side door behind the pulpit opened. Choir members filed in and took their seats. The piano player began "Nearer, My God, to Thee." The congregation rose.

Lammie turned to look down the aisle. The pews were full now and overflowed. Men stood around the sides of the sanctuary. Even the narthex was crowded.

She saw Pastor Mitchell in the doorway. He wore a suit, not a robe. They didn't hold with robes and such at Silver Creek. He waited, maybe for the family members to gather themselves, maybe for the piano to get through a chorus, then led them in. Cubby was right behind him.

Lammie held her breath. Taller than she remembered. Had he grown after he left town? Military posture. Tanned face. Slender with broad shoulders. He'd be strong under the midnight blue suit. His hair was still army short. Difficult to tell the color. It had been mid-brown. Maybe darker now. No gray?

His aunt Dru leaned on his arm. They both looked straight ahead, gazes fixed on the preacher's back. Lammie could have touched him as he went by her. Did his eyes shift just as he passed her? Did he glimpse her? Did he sense her? The starched collar of his shirt hid the freckles. She smiled behind her program.

He helped Dru to the middle of the front-most pew. A gaggle of people Lammie didn't know ("Camille's sister and her family. Cousins on the Tatum side," Helen or Freda whispered) took the pew behind Cubby and in front of

Lammie. They blocked her view.

"Let us pray."

The service moved apace. Three hymns, four prayers. Old Testament, New Testament, a eulogy from the gray-haired preacher who'd known the family since he was a young man just out of seminary. He went through Bear and Camille's meeting and marriage, the late-in-life birth of their only son, Bear building his insurance business, always with a mind to service, his time as county commissioner and mayor, his lasting legacy including the park by the lake he'd donated land for, and Littleboro's motto, The Little Town Time Forgot.

"I visited him often in the last weeks," Pastor Mitchell said. "A man whose faith never wavered. Neither should ours. We will see him again in Heaven. Let us pray."

After the prayer and before the benediction, the preacher said, "We'll move to the graveside, those who are able. And then the ladies of the church will serve lunch in the fellowship hall. The family hopes to greet you all then."

The pianist played "Eternal Father, Strong to Save."

No one moved while the casket was wheeled down the aisle and out of the chapel. Then Cubby, Dru, and the cousins filed by. The ushers tried to have Lammie's row go next, just as she had hoped they would, but people paid no attention, and she lost time while the overflow congregation sorted itself.

She trod on any feet that got in her way and elbowed as necessary to get out of the church. She meant to get to the grave site ahead of as many people as possible, to be near Cubby.

From the front steps, she saw Cubby hand Dru off to a cousin and join other men to bear the casket across the still-winter-brown grass. Their destination was a green canopy on top of a rise at the far side of the cemetery. The nearby trees were beginning to bud out and had a vague pink glow to them.

Some of the congregants were already easing toward the brick fellowship hall rather than go up the hill. Lammie could now be polite, respectful, and still gain ground. The midday air was cooler than the church had been, so she draped her jacket over her shoulders.

A funeral home man directed the able-bodied to stand while the family and elderly sat in folding chairs under the canopy. Lammie could not get as near Cubby as she wanted, but she had a clear view of him. He kept his head lowered, maybe staring at the casket resting at the grave's edge, badly disguised by vivid green artificial grass carpets. The Gone but Not Forgotten wreath was propped at the head of the casket, its frame not quite sitting level.

The headstone was ready to have the date of death added next to Camille's name and dates, under the inscription Reunited in Heaven.

It wasn't until then Lammie felt the slam of loss. Not the loss of Bear Tatum, but of her own daddy, George Timmons. He was buried in another country churchyard near his parents' farm. The only service had been at the graveside. No arrangements of white flowers. No piano, choir, or hymns. No carpets hiding the hole in the ground. Two stoic parents, a confused little girl, and a weeping widow saw his plain coffin into the earth, along with a few neighbors who'd known Daddy as a boy. Lammie swallowed hard, pulled the jacket up over her cheeks to catch tears.

The preacher prayed some more, commending Bear's soul to the Lord's keeping, calling down comfort and mercy for the loved ones left behind. And then it was time to file back down the hill.

When Lammie stepped inside the fellowship hall, it was already ringing with the voices of people released from the need to be hushed. It smelled of Brunswick stew in a row of Crock-Pots and coffee. Lammie knew to expect the long tables, the plates of deviled eggs, pimento cheese sandwiches with the crusts cut off, rolls and biscuits, bowls of fruit salad, cakes and pies. She knew to expect the mood to have lifted. It was how funerals went, but this time, seeing Mama, Helen, and Freda were already seated at a table with full plates in front of them, it sickened her a little.

Mama waved her over, and she went but didn't listen to or answer their questions. Attorney Morton and his wife came to say hello. He declared it a fine service, healing, the send-off Bear deserved. Lammie excused herself to get a glass of tea and stand by the door.

The cousins and Dru came in, were absorbed in well-wishers' embraces, then swept away to be given nourishment. Cubby was not with them. He must have lingered at the grave, a few more minutes alone with his father's casket. She should find her daddy's grave—it had been years since she even thought of it.

Finally, the door opened again, and there he was. Cubby. No one else saw him. Lammie took a few steps forward, and he looked right at her. The two of them. Alone in the crowd. His hazel eyes were clear and flickered a little when he saw her. Her cheeks warmed.

"Hello, Lammie," he said. "Thank you for being here."

"Hello, Cubby." They might have been six years old again, greeting each other as they had in first grade. She held out her hand, and he took it in both of his.

"Welcome home," she said.

And then the preacher claimed him, and he had to let go, but she knew he didn't want to. He held her gaze even as he turned. "See you soon, Lammie."

3

Lammie and Mama stood by their car, Helen and Freda beside theirs, while they waited for the church parking lot to clear.

"Y'all come to my house for supper," Freda said. "I have another chicken casserole I can thaw, and you can bring some side dishes. Just not succotash, Mary Ruth."

Mama sniffed and looked away.

"What time do you want us?" Helen asked.

"It's one thirty now. Let's say six o'clock. That gives you time to get to the store." She looked at Mama when she said that.

"I have work to do this afternoon, not shopping and cooking," Mama said. "What about you, Lammie? You going to the office?"

Lammie shook her head. "Attorney Morton says we're closed for the day."

"That Quinn turned out so handsome," Freda said. "It was hard to keep from calling him Cubby, though."

"So sweet to Dru. I feel better about her now," Helen said.

Lammie tuned them out. She had no plans to go to Freda's for supper. "Mama, I think we can get out now."

They got in the car, and Lammie backed out of the parking space.

"It would serve them right if I did take succotash." Mama dug in her pocketbook for Dentyne and offered Lammie a piece. "Stop at the Piggly Wiggly, and I'll buy some potato salad."

Lammie ignored the gum. She eased out onto the county road, into the line of cars heading back to town. They passed the Welcome to Littleboro sign. It was white with a silhouette of the courthouse in black. The motto the preacher had mentioned was painted in red script in an arc. Lammie wondered, Is it a good thing to be the town time forgot?

She read the Life and Time magazines in the reception area of the law office. She knew what she was missing. And she knew why she had stayed all this time.

"Lammie," Mama said, "you never did date Cubby—Quinn—did you?"

"No, but we were friends since kindergarten."

"If he stays in town, you ought to see what you can do. He'd be a catch. Rich, too, with all his daddy's money and property."

If he stayed in town. There was that to think about. He'd have to stay at least for a little while to tend to the estate. And surely he'd have to come to the law office. Maybe Lammie should call him—not tomorrow, too soon—but Monday, to see if he wanted an appointment with Attorney Morton.

It was easy to ignore Mama the rest of the drive home.

"Would you put the potato salad in the fridge?" Mama asked. "I need to get to work if I'm going to meet my Friday deadlines."

Lammie went to the kitchen to put away the food. Mama went straight to the dining room where she kept her adding machine and the ledger books for her bookkeeping clients spread out on the round oak table.

Lammie dawdled until she heard the adding machine keys clacking and knew there wouldn't be more conversation for a while. She went upstairs. She opened her closet door, slid the hanging garments to the left and right to create a gap in the middle, and stepped between them. Behind the clothes was a low door, a door built for a little girl by her father. "It's a secret playhouse, just for you, Lammie." Only she and he knew it was there.

Daddy loved to build things. "He wanted to be a carpenter," Granny told her once, "but he needed to make more money than carpenters get paid so he could marry your mama and have a little girl."

That's why he moved to Littleboro and went to work for Tatum Insurance Agency. That's where he met Mama, who worked there as a bookkeeper.

"He was so successful," Mama liked to tell people. "He'd have become a partner one day. If only, if only..." And she'd sniff like she wanted to cry.

Lammie studied the faces of the people Mama said that to. Did they believe it? Did she? Or was it another one of Mama's inventions?

The house at 305 Maple Street wasn't finished when Daddy bought it, so nights and weekends, he worked on it himself, including the secret room accessible only through Lammie's closet. He built shelves on its walls and a table and chair just big enough for a little girl.

Lammie ducked through the low door, turned on the light, and her shoulders relaxed. She kept some old dolls and children's books on the shelves, along with her high school yearbook and a small Samsonite suitcase Aunt Serena had given her on her eighteenth birthday. But most important, she had a row of shoeboxes that took up five feet of shelving. It was those boxes she visited when she needed to know everything would be all right.

She took one down, sat in the adult-sized chair she'd long since moved into the room, opened the box, and ran her fingers across the top edges of the dollar bills packed inside it. Ones, fives, tens. She raised the box toward her face and breathed deeply. This one held the oldest bills. After a while, they lost the smell of printing machines, cash drawers, leather wallets, and ladies' lavender-scented purses. The money just smelled like itself. Like nothing else she knew. Pure, somehow.

What would Cubby say if he knew she had this money, that she'd long ago decided it would be for the two of them, for the future she knew they'd share? Once he came back to Littleboro, once she told him—all these years she'd been here for him—he'd love her as much as she loved him.

4

Over the weekend, Lammie was restless. Saturday night, she didn't sleep, slipped into the secret room, and sat for a while.

Sunday morning, she pretended to sleep through Mama calling her to get ready for church. Spent the afternoon doing her laundry and took a nap.

"Don't you want to watch Columbo?" Mama asked after supper. "Or Cher. You pick."

"I need to wash my hair and iron my blouses for the week." Lammie headed upstairs.

"I wish you'd keep me company," Mama called.

Lammie went into her room and closed the door. The room was still painted pink, the color her daddy had chosen for his little girl. When she was in high school, Mama said, "We need to get you new curtains and a bedspread. That'll be your birthday this year."

Lammie didn't want a new bedspread. She used a quilt Granny had made. And the thread-bare white curtains with pink rosebuds made her think of Daddy, so when they went to the fabric store, she chose new material as near to the old as she could find.

Mama fussed, "Don't you want something more grownup?" But Lammie told her she'd pay for it herself from her babysitting money if Mama didn't like it. Now, all these years later, the room was still unchanged. Nothing was going to change until everything did.

She turned out the overhead light and went to the rocking chair by the window, the chair Daddy sat in to read bedtime stories to her. She raised the blinds and looked out over the street. She'd lived in this house, slept in this room, since she was three years old. Watched the tree Daddy planted grow. ("Lammie, we live on Maple Street. We've got to have a maple tree.") Watched Miss Leora's white house get painted yellow, then white again. The town installed streetlights, and children who lived on the street played in the new pools of light. When their mothers called them in, they hollered back, "It's not dark yet."

Lammie had not played with them because of what happened there in the yard where the light shone. Daddy had died just exactly there. And she had watched it from this window. She choked off the memory, like cinching a bag with a cord.

All those children were grown and gone. She was still there in her pink bedroom. Well, there had been the eleven months when she had a job in Raleigh and thought she'd escaped Littleboro. But look how that had ended. Right back where it started.

She closed her eyes and thought about Cubby. She'd thought about him a million times since high school graduation, thought about him while sitting here or in the secret room or during her walk to and from work. But now he was near, in that big house ten miles out of town.

The look he'd given her after the funeral, when he'd taken her hand, when he'd said "Hello, Lammie." His eyes soft and intense at once. And she'd see him again soon—soon. He'd said so. That was a thought she wasn't accustomed to.

No wonder she couldn't sleep.

Monday was just another Monday. She walked to work, stopped at the post office, went to the law office, made coffee, then sat down at her desk. She found the telephone book and looked up the number for the Tatum house. When Attorney Morton arrived, she would ask if he wanted her to call Cubby and schedule an appointment.

But Attorney Morton wasn't there at nine o'clock, or at ten after. At twenty past, the door opened.

"Look who I ran into." Attorney Morton stepped aside, and Cubby walked through the door. "He was getting his breakfast at the Legal Eagle, said he needed to come meet with me, and I said no time like the present."

Cubby's eyes focused on Lammie and widened. She held her breath.

Attorney Morton crossed to her desk and set down the white paper sack with her cinnamon roll and his sausage biscuit. Lammie stood up and then didn't know what to do. Run to Cubby, as she wanted to?

"Hello, Lammie." Cubby was close now and held out his hand. Just the way he had in the church fellowship hall.

"Hello, Cubby."

Simple words anybody would say to anybody else, but they meant something special to the two of them.

"Come on in, Quinn," Attorney Morton said. "Lammie, I bet our client would accept a cup of coffee."

Cubby's fingertips lingered on hers. Then he followed Attorney Morton into his office. Lammie took a moment to collect herself, then went to get the coffee. She fit two filled cups, a sugar bowl, creamer, and spoons on a tray as she had done hundreds of times. She was shaky carrying it, and the coffee sloshed a little as she put it down on Attorney Morton's desk.

"I have the original will," Cubby was saying. "Dad made sure Aunt Dru knew where everything was. In case I didn't make it in time." He glanced up at Lammie.

"It was a blessing you were there at the end," Attorney Morton said. "You'll treasure that. Lammie, did you need something?"

"I could go with you to the clerk's office," she said to Cubby. "To file the will."

"I'd appreciate it," he said. "The army didn't teach me this stuff."

"All right, then." Attorney Morton cleared his throat.

He didn't matter. His dismissal didn't count for anything.

Back at her desk, something rose from deep inside Lammie. She couldn't stop it. All she could do was sit still, wait, wait, until it broke forth. Sobs and tears.

Tears? She'd left crying behind years ago.

She couldn't let her boss or Cubby see her like this. She grabbed her purse and ran to the ladies' room down the corridor. Thank goodness nobody was in it. She locked the cubicle door and went through half a roll of tissue trying to staunch the tears, the snot.

Then it was long minutes of bathing her face with cool water, gazing at her eyes in the mirror, searching for signs, searching for clarity while the red faded, the swelling receded. She rescued her makeup as best she could with what she carried in a cosmetics pouch. Her hair was inexplicably messy. She dampened her hands and smoothed it.

Her ankles wobbled as she went back down the hall. Attorney Morton's door was closed. She couldn't hear voices.

The white bag was gone, but the cinnamon roll wrapped in waxed paper sat in the middle of her blotter, along with a folded sheet of paper. A note from Cubby. "Dear Lammie, would you be able to help me file the will on Friday? I would be happy to take you to lunch, if you have time."

Oh, she'd have time.

5

On Friday, Lammie wore her newest suit, one she'd bought on sale at the end of the last summer season. These March days were seeing highs in the seventies, much warmer than normal, so a mid-weight polished cotton was fine for the weather. Skirt just above the knees, a two-button jacket. Navy blue with dark pink piping on the lapels and sleeve cuffs. She wore a lighter pink blouse. The pearl earrings. And underneath it all, pink silk bra, panties, and slip. Cubby wouldn't know that, but she'd learned long ago that the lingerie she kept wrapped in tissue and hidden in Aunt Serena's suitcase made her feel good, even under the dowdiest clothes. Her secrets were her greatest comforts.

She was to meet Cubby on the courthouse steps at eleven o'clock. She was there early and watched the white Cadillac that had belonged to Mr. Bear circle the square. It stopped, parked, and there he was. Cubby. Again. First at the church, then in the fellowship hall, then in the office, and now, coming her way.

He wore a blue sports coat, tan slacks, a white shirt, and a blue-and-white-striped tie. One thing Lammie could agree with Mama about was, it was sad people didn't care how they dressed anymore. And those hippies? Thank goodness people in Littleboro had better sense, but still, don't go to the Piggly Wiggly on Saturday mornings unless you want a shock. Nice to know Cubby made efforts.

And as good as he looked in his clothes, he'd look even better without them. Would his skin be soft? Maybe he would let her rub lotion onto his back. Lammie didn't even blush at the thought.

He caught sight of her and began to walk faster. He trotted up the steps.

"This is kind of you, Lammie," he said.

She stifled her fantasy. "Happy to do it, of course."

He stepped past her and opened the heavy double door. "Lead the way."

The courthouse lobby was marble and brass with mahogany trim work. Wide stairs invited visitors to ascend to the second floor, where the oak-paneled courtroom was.

"We go this way." Lammie took the corridor to the left. It narrowed and darkened and led to a series of offices behind wooden doors identified with gold lettering. The third one on the right was Registrar and Probate.

Lammie had been through that door more times than she could count with paperwork for Attorney Morton's clients. Never had she entered with a man, much less a handsome, nicely dressed man. The women who worked there were going to sit up straighter when she walked in with Cubby. They'd wish they'd done more about their own appearance that morning, wish they'd known to take time with their hair and add a swipe of lipstick ten minutes earlier.

"Good morning, Esther," Lammie said. "Do you know Mr. Tatum? He's here to file his father's will."

Esther Pritchett stood and smoothed her skirt. "Of course, Mr. Tatum. Your father was such a fine man. Such a loss. Let's go into my office."

"I appreciate that, Esther. And I remember your own parents from church when I was a boy."

Esther looked to Lammie, probably expecting her to depart now she'd shown Cubby in. Lammie smiled at her and preceded them both into the clerk's small office.

Esther sat behind the desk and explained Cubby's duties as executor and the schedule he needed to follow. Lammie weighed in from time to time, "Attorney Morton and I can tend to that one, if you want."

Esther frowned and stared over her half-glasses at Lammie. Lammie smiled.

An hour later, Lammie and Cubby stood on the courthouse steps again. The sun was high, shining in Lammie's eyes. She felt his hand on her elbow. Anybody seeing them would think, those two make a handsome couple.

"Do you have time for lunch?" he asked.

"That would be nice."

"Is the Legal Eagle OK? You'd think this town would have another restaurant by now."

"Maybe you haven't heard. We're the town time forgot."

It was a risk, given his father's fingerprints on that motto. But he laughed. "I heard that."

They stopped by the Cadillac so he could leave off his papers. Just inside the front door of the café, people jostled for space.

"Half these people are waiting on takeout," Lammie said. She looked over the shoulders of people in front of them and saw the owner, Mr. Huey, working the cash register. She waved.

"Hey, Lammie. Is that Quinn Tatum with you?" Mr. Huey came from behind his counter and shook Cubby's hand. "Son, I miss your daddy. He ate breakfast here three times a week for so many years. A great man. Y'all take the booth by the window."

Lammie turned her back on any dirty looks from people ahead of them and slid onto the seat. Cubby settled across from her.

Before they could order, or even get waters and silverware sets, three more people had stopped to speak to Cubby, to declare their admiration for Mr. Bear, and to reminisce. Cubby stood up each time, shook hands, nodded, thanked them, sat again, only to stand again, sit again.

"It's like being here with a movie star," Lammie said.

"Can I tell you a secret?" He leaned toward her across the table.

Before she could lean forward to hear it, a waitress named Callie appeared. "What can I get for you?"

Cubby ordered the catfish sandwich with slaw. Lammie ordered a chicken salad plate. They both ordered tea, hers sweet, his not.

"A shot or two of bourbon would be better," Cubby said when the waitress was gone. "It wasn't easy, hearing my dad's death turned into process and procedure. Life reduced to the stuff and the money left over. It meant a lot, having you there."

He leaned forward again. "But Lammie, I swear to God, if one more person tells me how good my dad was, I'm going to punch something."

She sat back. This was more than a small secret.

"My dad—behind closed doors—he was a son of a bitch." Cubby's jawline sharpened, neck muscles taut. His eyes turned the color of flint. On the table, his fists clinched.

Maybe he told everybody these things. Or maybe he had never—until now—said it out loud. If the one, then it meant nothing. If the other, it meant everything. It meant she'd been right to wait and believe.

She drew in a breath and held it. "I never knew."

"Nobody knew. They all thought—" He waved his hand to encompass the world where Bear Tatum was a hero. "Well, Mom. She shielded me best she could, but why do you think I left the way I did and never came back? She always visited me, wherever I was stationed, except Vietnam. And she told me it was OK to stay away. When she died so suddenly, I was in a jungle. Couldn't get here. That's my only regret." He looked her in the eyes.

"And Aunt Dru, of course, she knew. She grew up with him. Says he was a mean kid. But even so, she moved in after Mom died to help Dad out. She didn't have to stay. Not like Mom did. Or thought she did. If he got too ugly, Dru could pack a bag and go stay with her friend for a while. When she came back, he'd be full of sweetness for a few weeks. She laid down some rules, and she says he actually treated her decently. I hope so."

All that said in a level voice. No hesitation. This was getting air for the first time. He'd been waiting to tell somebody. To tell her.

How could she not have known this about Mr. Bear when she'd watched Cubby so closely since they were five?

"Did he—what did he do?"

"Did he hit me? Spankings when I was little. His hand, a belt, a paddle. When I got older, bigger, I wished he would so I could hit him back. But mostly he bullied. I was never good enough. Not big enough for football. Track didn't mean squat. Not good at math. How was I going to work in his business if I couldn't do math? He told me, bragged, he was sleeping with senior girls when he was a high school freshman. Had I ever been with a girl? Would I ever? Was I queer?"

"But you dated the prettiest girls." And it had hurt to see them, one after another, on his arm. Every time he broke up with one, Lammie had hoped, this time, he'd turn around and see her waiting.

"According to Dad, if they'd go out with me, there had to be something wrong with them."

Their food came. They ate, didn't talk, didn't hurry even while the crowd around them shifted and changed. People on their lunch hour ate fast, paid, and left. Late-comers bustled in. Lammie watched Cubby eat his sandwich like it was the best thing he'd tasted in a while, like every fry needed his full attention. Or was he wishing he hadn't told her? Is that why he studied his plate and didn't look at her anymore?

Noise from the kitchen lessened. The waitresses began to wipe down tables as they emptied. Mr. Huey sat behind his cash register, arms crossed. He wanted to close out.

"They stop serving at two," Lammie said. Attorney Morton would have gone home to lunch. He'd be back by now, wondering where she was. There were appointments on the calendar. Cubby used his last fry to wipe a dab of ketchup off his plate.

"It's been a while since I could take my time with a meal. Even just a sandwich at the Legal Eagle." He sat back and looked at her again. The flint softened to hickory nut green. "Lammie, I shouldn't have laid all that on you."

"Yes, you should have." Now she was the one leaning in. "You can trust me. I keep secrets."

"I guess it's because I've known you so long—you were always there, weren't you?"

Does the sun know what its warmth feels like on the face of somebody who has been cold forever?

She nodded.

"I want to see you again," he said. "Not for business."

"Mama is going to visit her sister tomorrow. She'll be gone overnight. You could come over."

"Aunt Dru needs me in the morning, but I can probably get away later. Do you still live on Maple Street?"

"Number 305. I'll be home all day."

6

That night, Mama cooked supper, moved her work off the dining room table, and set their places with the nice dishes. She made smothered chicken, egg noodles, and steamed broccoli with almonds sprinkled on top. Efforts like this set Lammie's teeth on edge.

"It's nice, Mama."

"Don't I always set a nice table? What do you want to drink?"

"What are you having?"

They both knew what was in Mama's tall glass. Ice, water, bourbon. She'd have poured the first one an hour earlier, topped it off a time or two while at the stove. But she looked at it as if surprised.

"I'll take care of myself," Lammie said.

She fixed a glass of ice water. Mama frowned at it, at her. If Mama kept drinking, she'd eventually say, "I won't be judged in my own house by my own daughter." Like Lammie's ice water was a judgement.

Too bad.

Mama talked about the weather, a little gossip she'd picked up making her rounds on business that day, including, "Mr. Huey said you came in for lunch today with Quinn Tatum."

"That's right."

"I told you, you ought to see about him. What's he planning to do with Mr. Bear's rental properties?"

"You know I can't talk about one of Attorney Morton's clients."

There was ice cream for dessert, but neither of them wanted any. Mama topped off her glass once more and turned on the TV. Lammie washed the dishes. She looked hard at Mama's bottle, decided to suit herself, and poured an ounce of bourbon into a high ball glass. She added ice cubes and swished them to let them start melting.

"I'm tired, Mama." Lammie went upstairs with her glass. She got ready for bed, then went into the secret room. It was Friday. On Fridays, she added the week's collections to a shoebox and added up the new total in a notebook. This week, she had thirty dollars, on the low side. The new total was $87,940.

Before she left the space, she picked up her high school yearbook from senior year, one of the treasures she kept on a shelf there.

She propped up in bed, sipped her drink, and held a romance novel open on her stomach until she heard Mama come up and go to bed about ten o'clock. Sometimes, Mama tapped on her door, opened it a little, and called, "Night-night." Sometimes, she took a few steps into the room. Then it was Lammie who said, "Night, Mama," to head off chitchat. And sometimes, like tonight, neither of them spoke.

When she heard Mama's bedroom door close, Lammie set the novel aside and opened the yearbook.

When she moved back home from a year living in Raleigh and started work for Attorney Morton, she had almost thrown the yearbook away. Anything that reminded her of the past added to her disgrace, her failure. But she'd opened it one more time to look at the comments classmates had written under their portraits or on the back pages left blank for that purpose.

Bernard Quinn Tatum Jr. had done both. He'd scribbled "Quinn" over his face. In the back of the book, he wrote, "To my oldest friend, Lammie. Thanks for having my back—ha ha—since kindergarten. Don't forget me when you go out into the big world." He signed it, "Till we meet again, your friend forever, Cubby."

His handwriting was neat, precise, the way they'd both learned to write in elementary school. She ran a finger over the words.

On graduation night, a few kids had cried, but most of them were happy, ready to be out of high school, ready to jump into life, or maybe just to get the hell out of Littleboro. What she remembered, as she sat there with the book open almost twenty-one years later, was Amanda Pruitt bawling in the girls' room before the ceremony. Amanda, everybody knew, went steady with Cubby. Lammie asked somebody what Amanda was upset about, and the answer was—Cubby's enlisted. He's going into the army next week, and Amanda didn't know until he'd told her just now.

That was how Lammie herself found out. Amanda was surrounded by friends who tried to comfort her, who told her it was an awful thing Cubby did to her. Lammie leaned against the tile wall, alone in the crowd of girls.

Her heart seized up at the words enlisted and next week. Never mind Amanda Pruitt. How could Cubby not have told her, when she'd loved him for so long? Lammie had to choke down tears all by herself.

Less than three years later, that first night home from Raleigh, exiled, her shame as tender as burned flesh, Lammie reread Cubby's message to her. Till we meet again. Your friend forever. And just like that, she knew. He would come home, maybe in another year or two when he got out of the army, and he'd find her there. And this time, he would look at her differently, see that he'd loved her all along.

She had carried the yearbook into her secret space, laid it on a shelf, and made a promise, her hand on it as if on a Bible: she'd wait for him.

But he didn't come home in a year or two. Instead, he made the army his life for more than twenty years. Lammie went to high school reunions and heard people wonder, will Quinn ever come home? Amanda Pruitt came with her husband, some man she'd met in college, and Lammie watched her hugging her friends, laughing, telling stories, acting like she'd never cried on graduation night. Lammie always left the party early, went home, and pulled out the yearbook.

When Littleboro built a park on a lake outside of town, on land Bear Tatum donated, Lammie sometimes drove out there and sat on a bench by the water. When the leaves were off the trees, she could see the Tatums' big house on a hill across the lake. But now, two decades later, Cubby was finally home in that house.

Lammie's room was stuffy. She got up and went to the window, thinking she could open it an inch or two. It was a dangerous thing to do. Memories tended to blow in with the night air. She heard dogs bark in the distance. When she pulled the closed curtains apart a few inches, she saw the blue glow in Miss Leora's front-room window. Her TV was on as usual. Lammie imagined Miss Leora falling asleep in front of it and waking up to the sound of her own snores.

Miss Leora had been there the night Daddy died. She'd once whispered to Lammie, "If you have any questions about what happened that night, you can come to me."

Lammie was in high school then. Miss Leora must have thought she was old enough. Maybe she knew Mama didn't talk about it, or when she did, she lied.

But Lammie never asked, never intended to, and she avoided Miss Leora when she could. She knew what she remembered, what she had seen from that very window. Once when she was in the public library working on a term paper, she had asked the librarian if there were old newspapers. Yes, on microfiche. Lammie learned to use the awkward machine, slide the filmy sheets under the light, and read the fuzzy white-on-black words that reported on that night in July 1944. What more could Miss Leora tell her?

After that, when Miss Leora looked at her, Lammie felt transparent, felt known in a way she didn't want to be known. Not that Miss Leora wasn't kind, but Lammie didn't want kindness.

The dogs hushed. Got called inside, maybe. It was a neighborhood where people didn't want to disturb each other. Her drink was down to slushy sweet ice, the way she liked it. She felt the cold roll down to her gut. The next sip, she warmed in her mouth before swallowing. She gave herself permission to think about Cubby and what he'd told her about his father.

7

Next morning, Mama carried her little blue travel bag downstairs. "Are you sure you don't want to go with me? You haven't seen your Aunt Serena in months."

"Maybe next time."

"All right," Mama said. "You can't say I didn't offer."

"I would never say that. Have fun."

They looked at each other for a moment. Lammie had the feeling that Mama waited for her to say more.

Lammie nodded toward the bag. "I can carry that for you."

"This little thing? I think I can still manage. Not over the hill yet." Mama headed for the front door.

Lammie followed, stood on the porch, and watched her go. When the car turned off Maple onto Elm, she flung her arms out and inhaled as if the air was fresher, crisper, sweeter than two minutes earlier. Cubby would be coming soon.

She ran upstairs to change clothes. She went into the secret room, opened the Samsonite suitcase, and took out the tissue paper bundle that held her cream-colored satin bra and panties, the bra set with tiny pink ribbon rosettes. They were rose-scented from the soap she used to wash her nicest things.

She put the bra and panties on. She liked what she saw in the full-length mirror, turned to examine herself from all sides. Cubby would like it too. He would be a man who appreciated curves, softness, sweetness. She slid a loose-fitting winter-white knit dress over her head. The house was warm enough, she could go bare-legged. Taupe flats with pointed toes.

Hair down or up? It was thick and wavy, always went its own way eventually. She put it in a twist and clipped it up with a silver barrette. One touch and it would tumble down to her shoulders.

When would he come? She picked up her romance book, went downstairs, and got a glass of tea. She settled in a chair by the front window that gave her a view of the street. She slid her shoes off, opened the book across her lap, and riffled the pages with her thumb. The grandfather clock in the hall struck three. She took a deep breath and exhaled slowly.

Lammie had been to bed with three men in her life. The first time, she was sixteen and he was the husband of a woman she babysat for. He was a little drunk and driving her home one night, well, she was never quite sure how it happened, but it did, and in the end, she wasn't sorry. It was a secret to add to her small collection of secrets. The family moved away not long after that.

The second man was somebody she met while she was

going to business college. They got together in his tiny apartment after classes. When he graduated, he went back to his hometown and married his childhood sweetheart. Lammie had been afraid he'd want to marry her, so that was all right.

And there was the senator. Thoughts of him squirmed and kicked sometimes, but she kept them in the cinched bag of memories she couldn't look at in the light.

Cubby was coming. Why should any of those other men matter to her?

The doorbell woke her. She sat up and blinked while her mind cleared. She saw a car at the curb in front of the house. Bear Tatum's white Cadillac.

The bell rang again.

She let the book drop and ran to the front door barefooted. He stood at the edge of the porch, his back to her. He rocked on his heels, his hands in his pockets. The collar of a blue oxford-cloth shirt showed over the neck of a tan jacket. His pants were khaki, his loafers cordovan.

"Hey there," she said.

He turned around and smiled. She saw the boy behind the smile, behind the crinkles around his eyes.

"Hello, Lammie." He held out his hand. "I wasn't sure anybody was home."

"Come on in." She opened the screen door and stood aside.

He stepped past her, not quite brushing against her. She led the way into the front room, slid her feet into her shoes, and stooped to pick up her book.

He looked around. "I've been to your house before, right? High school?"

"I think so." She knew so. "Mama let me give a little

party once." And he'd come with Amanda Pruitt. "Please sit down."

"It's funny how things come back to you." He sat on the couch.

Lammie had talked to him in her mind and her dreams a million times, but now with him in front of her, she couldn't remember a single thing she'd meant to say. She should show concern about his grieving, even for a father he'd—was hated too strong a word? She should ask how his aunt was doing. But where were those words?

"Would you like a glass of tea?"

"That would be nice."

She carried her own glass to the kitchen, set it down, and wiped her hands on a dish towel. Her lungs were constricted. She was too warm.

She took an ice cube tray from the freezer, fumbled with it. The cubes came loose all at once and clattered into the sink. One skittered across the countertop. She caught it and pressed it to the hollow of her throat.

"Can I help you, Lammie?" He was in the doorway.

The ice cube slipped from her fingers and down into the loose-fitting dress. It left a cool trail between her breasts, over her tummy, and hit the floor at her feet.

"I didn't mean to startle you," he said.

"That's all right." She bent to pick up the chunk of ice, and he bent toward it too. They avoided bumping heads, and it was she who raised up with the cube in her hand. She felt a giggle rising from the pit of her stomach and tried to squelch it, but it erupted, and tears flowed right behind it. Again? Where were all the damned tears coming from?

"Do you need to sit down?" Cubby took her elbows and eased her into a kitchen chair. "Are you OK?" He took the ice cube from her and tossed it into the sink.

She pressed her fingers against the bridge of her nose. Cubby found a paper napkin somewhere, squeezed it into her hand. When she opened her eyes, he was kneeling in front of her. He was concerned, worried, puzzled. His face was close, smooth from a recent shave. His aftershave, citrus and spice. She twisted her fingers in her skirt.

"You're upset about something," he said. "Should I go?"

"Oh no." The thought of him leaving dried her eyes.

She leaned forward and kissed him. He pulled away, looked at her as if she was a stranger, but then came back and returned the kiss. She rested one hand on the back of his neck, where the constellation of freckles lay. He took her elbows again and they stood up, pressed together. They kissed again, and he held her waist, then her hips. He kissed her neck, her ear. Then stopped.

"This is not what I expected," he whispered. "Not what I came for."

It was happening. "Would you like to come upstairs?"

She led the way. The daylight was filtered through curtain sheers, muted. Even though they were alone in the house, she closed the bedroom door behind them.

Three hours later, they sat on the screened porch at the back of the house, sharing the glider with an afghan over their knees, and looking out over the backyard. It would be dark soon.

They had hardly spoken since they came downstairs. When they went through the kitchen, Lammie had asked, did he want a drink? He said yes. She took an ice cube tray out of the freezer.

"Maybe I should do this," he'd said. They both laughed a little. He levered the cubes out of their cells and put them in two tall glasses. She poured ginger ale and bourbon. She found a can of salted peanuts, a box of Triscuits, and a wedge of hoop cheese. They carried all of that out to the porch.

Lammie sipped her drink and ate three peanuts. Her nerves—tingling after their love-making—settled in a low hum.

After a while, Cubby said, "It's nice back here. Quiet. You can't even see the neighbors' houses."

She turned toward him, lifted a hand, and touched his face. "It is nice. With you."

He took her hand. "When I saw you at the funeral, I remembered you'd always been pretty. And smart. And I thought, I'd like to know what she's been up to."

When had anybody asked her that question? Never that she could remember.

"You truly want to know about me?"

He nodded. "I wonder why you're still in Littleboro."

She took a deep breath in, exhaled slowly. "I always thought I'd get away from here, like you did, but not to go so far, I guess. After high school, I drove to Raleigh every day and took classes at a business college to be a legal secretary. Then I got an apartment with another girl and took a job in state government."

"Why a legal secretary?"

"I don't know. I looked at a list of courses and certificates, and it was different. I thought, if I liked it, maybe I would be a lawyer." She shrugged. "Sometimes my boss says I should be the one with the diploma."

"Well? Why don't you have one?"

"Girls didn't do that back then. It was a silly idea. I'm doing fine."

"But you're still in Littleboro. You wanted to get away."

"That part is harder to explain. Anyway, aren't you glad I'm here?"

"I guess I am." He kissed her temple.

"You need another drink?"

"Let me get them." He stood up and took her glass from her. "Don't go anywhere."

Then he was back, handing her a glass, resettling the afghan, putting his arm around her shoulders.

"There's something I want to ask you," she said.

"Ask me anything."

She took a deep breath. "I wonder, what do you know about how my daddy died?"

He tensed, but his arm stayed. "I don't remember much. How old were you?"

"Six. It was the summer before first grade." She set her drink on the coffee table and shifted to face him. "Do you know, he worked for your father?"

"I think I knew that. I think I remember my folks talking about it—but it was the kind of thing, they'd stop if I came in the room."

"It was that kind of thing." She looked out into the dark yard for a moment, then back to him. "I've never told anybody what I saw that night."

She took a deep breath and began. It had been a hot night. The bedrooms in the house didn't have air conditioners, so her window was open with a fan. She was asleep. And then she woke up because there was yelling, a man yelling outside the house. She got out of bed and went to the window. She had to peek around the edge of the fan. A man was in the front yard, yelling. At Daddy. Daddy was in the yard. He was barefooted. He had his hands up. He was talking, but he wasn't yelling back. Daddy was calm, always calm. The man had driven there, and his car was parked at the curb, the front door open so the inside light was on. He went to his car and got something. It was a shotgun, and he shot Daddy with both barrels.

"My God, Lammie. Why?" Cubby sat so still.

"I didn't know for a long time. Not until I found the old newspapers at the library. He thought Daddy was having an affair with his wife. She worked with Daddy at your father's insurance company. The man thought that, so he killed Daddy."

"And you saw it all."

"I couldn't take it in. The noise was awful, the yelling, the booms, then lots more voices. Mama screaming. Sirens. Lights. All I could do was crawl back in bed and pull up the covers and hide my head under my pillow.

"In a while, my door opened. I stayed as still as I could. I heard two people—one was our neighbor, Miss Leora—and they said, looks like she's asleep. Wouldn't that be a blessing, if she slept through it all? The sleep of the innocent. We can tell Mary Ruth she's fine, she's safe.

"They closed my door. I slipped out of bed again and went back to the window. The man who'd shot Daddy was sitting on the ground beside the maple tree with his head down. Two policemen stood beside him. The ambulance crew—I know now that's who they must have been—were bending over Daddy on the ground. I couldn't see Mama, but I heard her. Crying, screaming, then hushing, then crying. I think some neighbors probably had her on the front porch. Out of the way. Holding onto her.

"Over all these years, she's believed I was asleep the whole time because Miss Leora told her that. Lammie doesn't remember a thing, thank the Lord, Mama'll say. We've never talked about it. And I've never told her or anybody the truth."

"What happened to the man?" Cubby shifted to face her.

"That's another thing I didn't know for a long time. And couldn't ask. When I moved back from Raleigh and went to work for Attorney Morton, I went to the courthouse and looked it up. There was a trial. The man went to prison, but not for long. A crime of passion. Defending his wife, his home. Not in his right mind, they said."

Cubby had hold of her now, both arms around her. "Lammie, it's awful. I don't know how you stood it, keeping all that inside."

They stayed as they were for a long time. They had been skin to skin, hot and needy, for hours. But this, with clothes on, the afghan tangled between their legs, this was where Lammie melted into him and he into her.

Finally, Cubby said it. "I should go. Aunt Dru will be looking for me. She isn't used to being alone in the house yet." But he didn't move.

And then they made love on the glider, Aunt Dru and March breezes be damned.

When they finally made their way through the house to the front porch, the streetlights were on, and the neighbors' living room windows glowed. Lammie and Cubby kissed almost chastely, aware of there being other people in the world.

"When do I see you again?" she whispered.

"What time do you get off work Friday?" he asked.

Not until Friday? "Five o'clock."

"I'll pick you up at your office." He held onto her hand as he backed down the steps, as if he didn't want to let go.

She watched until the Cadillac's taillights disappeared.

The grandfather clock rang nine times. Lammie poured herself one more drink and carried it to her bedroom. She breathed in the scent she and Cubby had left. Tomorrow, before Mama got home, she'd wash the sheets. But tonight, she'd revel in them.

She took a long sip, then went through the hidden door at the back of the closet. She took one of the shoeboxes off the shelf and out into the bedroom. She sat in the chair by the window and opened it. This one held her twenty-dollar bills.

She had thought of showing Cubby the money that night. Of course she had. They'd been so close to it, she could imagine it rustling while they made love. But something told her it was too soon. She would know when the time was right. She imagined how surprised he'd be. And how happy. Their future together secured.

8

When Joe Corcoran's dad died, three years after his mom, Joe decided to hit the road. Go with his gut. No destination, no plan.

He sold his car and his dad's car, the little house he'd grown up in, and everything that didn't fit into the 1968 VW camper van he bought and refurbished. With money from the sales, plus his parents' savings and his own, he'd be all right for quite a while. People said he was crazy giving up a good job as a route salesman for the local Coca-Cola distributor.

What they didn't get was, he loved driving. What he didn't love was the part of his job that meant having to please the bosses and keep a tight schedule and not have time to stop and look at a rainbow or at black cows grazing in a green pasture. Now he didn't have Mom and Dad to worry about anymore; he was free to drive when and where he wanted, stop when he wanted, look at a map or not—suit himself.

Besides, all those retirees from up north were beginning to crowd into central Florida from both coasts. Like his dad used to say, it didn't seem like Florida was for Floridians anymore.

He left home two days after his forty-sixth birthday and headed west with no plan. When he got to the Mississippi River, he'd decide, cross it and keep going or follow it north for a while. Whatever his gut said, he'd do.

His second day out, on a little-traveled road in Arkansas, he came upon an old land-yacht station wagon broken down by the side of the road with a white handkerchief tied to the antenna. Must have been out of gas. If it was the engine, the hood would be up. A man stood by the car, and when he saw the camper van approach, he yanked the cap off his head and waved it like crazy.

Joe pulled over, sizing things up. A woman with a couple of young kids sat on a blanket on a little rise across a ditch from the man and the car. The kids both wore T-shirts and overalls. One was taller and had pigtails. A girl. She stuffed four fingers into her mouth when she saw Joe's camper van. The littler kid had short hair. A boy. The woman hung onto the seat of his pants, or he'd have run toward the road. Well sure, a boy wanted to be with the men.

"Hey." Joe rolled his window down. "Looks like you got problems."

"Yes, sir. Ran short of gas." The man stepped toward him. He was young, skinny, kind of funny looking with droopy hound dog eyes and a hawk nose. "There's a station a couple of miles back. Would you give me a lift?"

"I can do better than that." Joe stepped out of the van and went around to the back where he kept two five-gallon cans strapped on.

"Brother, you are a lifesaver." The man's voice loosened with relief.

"It makes sense to carry a little spare fuel when you're on the road," Joe said.

The man's downcast look made him sorry he'd said it. Likely the woman had already pointed that out. Plus, spare fuel took spare money, and not everybody could use a gas can for a piggy bank. When Joe carried the can to the car, he got a glimpse into the back. Looked like the family might be living there.

The boy child yelped and broke loose. He charged toward his daddy, who caught him and hoisted him to his shoulder, laughing. A good man, just on hard times.

Joe put the gas in the tank, refused the offer of money, and gave the little boy two candy bars. "You be sure your sister gets one."

When the woman came forward with the little girl holding her hand, Joe saw she carried a third kid, a baby who must have been sleeping on her lap before.

The man went to retrieve the blanket. While he was gone, Joe took one, then two, then three ten-dollar bills out of his wallet. The woman accepted them without a word, folded them, and tucked them into the top of her dress.

Joe thought a lot about those people for the rest of the day. They had shown him why he was out there. This was his mission. Helping people.

Over the next months, Joe changed flat tires, poured gas into tanks and water into radiators, gave rides and lectures to young people who ought not be thumbing rides. The world wasn't safe out there, didn't they know? Here in the '70s, things had gotten crazy. Not like when he was a kid.

He stopped in any town he passed through when he needed to find a laundromat, a barber shop, a grocery store. He camped in state parks, national parks, and church parking lots. He changed the van's oil and did routine maintenance, but after eight months and a lot of miles—the odometer had stopped working, not that it mattered—it was time to find a place where he could stay for a while, get the van cleaned up, fully serviced, and new tires. He wouldn't mind a few days in one place. Get his land legs back.

He passed a sign on the interstate that said, Raleigh Next Five Exits. Joe had never been there before, so going with his gut, he took the second exit.

The road he landed on was bordered by ragged-looking strip shopping centers, warehouses, and small industries. He'd seen the same many times, in many places. Not especially promising, until he saw a big lighted sign: Highway Home Hotel, free cable TV, suites with kitchenettes, and weekly rates.

He turned into the driveway to take a look. The hotel was a three-story building, long and narrow, set back from the road. Trees, mostly pines, bordered it on both sides. The windows across the second and third floors had fake shutters. Trying to look homey, like the name said.

Joe stopped at the front door. He got out of the camper van, stretched his back, hitched up his pants, and went in.

The carpet was faded red, green, yellow—maybe meant

to be an autumn leaf pattern. It was worn but clean. Joe headed for the reception desk he could see down the hall. He passed an elevator to his right, a loveseat and a pair of chairs in an alcove. The registration desk was unmanned.

Joe walked up to it and tapped on the bell in the middle of the counter. "Anybody home?" he called.

"Hi there." A door opened and a gawky young man appeared. "How you doing, sir?"

He had limp brown hair to his shoulders, the way kids wore it these days.

"Doing fine, thanks. Hoping you've got a nice, quiet room for me."

"Sure thing." The young man pulled a notebook out of a drawer, opened it, and laid it in front of Joe. "Our suites all have kitchenettes and living rooms. Color TV and cable for free. You a sports fan? It's great for watching sports."

Joe read the young man's name tag.

"Not too much, Terry. I'm on the road these days. In fact, you could say I'm a highway man."

"Yeah?" Terry smiled, but Joe could tell he didn't get it.

"We have daily, weekly, monthly rates." Terry pointed to the rate card posted under glass on the desktop. He turned the notebook around for Joe to sign in and handed him a ballpoint pen.

"Let's say a week," Joe said. He printed his name and his license plate number. "No home address. Is that a problem?"

"Nah. I get that pretty often. You pay cash, no problem." Terry studied the notebook, upside down. "Joe." He said that with confidence, then with uncertainty, "Cor-cor-an?"

"We say Cork-ran." Joe capped the pen and handed it back. He pulled out his wallet and held it down low so

Terry wouldn't see how much money was in it. He counted out the bills and laid a week's rent on top of the notebook.

"OK, Mr. Cor-cor-an. I'm giving you 312. I put all the weeklies and monthlies on the top floor so nobody's stomping around over your head. Quiet, like you say, except when the dumpster gets emptied, but that's only Tuesday and Friday afternoons. You'll have a nice view too." He held out a green plastic key fob with two keys on it. "There's only one other room on the third occupied right now."

"Sounds fine, Terry." Joe took the keys.

"Most of our guests use the front door and the front elevator, but for you, the back door will be more convenient." Terry pointed down a hallway that went past the desk to the rear of the building. "Just drive around and park where you want. You can bring your stuff in that way. Save yourself some steps. You'll see the service elevator, if you don't mind sharing with the cleaning ladies. Ice and vending machines are right beside it. I lock the door at ten o'clock. That second key, the silver one, it'll let you in if you're out late."

"I appreciate it. You're the night man, I guess."

"I'm here just about all the time. My uncle owns the place, and I live right there. Little apartment just like all our suites." He pointed to the door he'd come through. "You ring the bell or dial 0 on your phone anytime, and I'm likely to be the one who answers."

"Any place good to eat around here?"

"I like the Chinese in the shopping center next door. It's open until nine. The egg rolls are real good."

"Thanks, Terry. I'll check it out."

Joe took the elevator to the third floor so he could scope out the room before moving stuff in. Room 312 was to his left. He paused to look around. There was a fire door between the elevator and his room. Joe opened it and verified there was a staircase behind it. The housekeeper's closet was on the far side of the elevator. He checked the door. It wasn't locked. Shelves holding folded towels and sheets along with all kinds of cleaning supplies were nice and tidy. Because the stairwell, the elevator, and the closet took up space, there was only one other room on the narrow backside of the building, Room 314.

Once he had the place mapped out, Joe unlocked 312. When he flipped a light switch, a floor lamp came on. A big TV on a console sat against one wall. A low, modern-style couch covered in rough-looking green upholstery was opposite it. A heavy coffee table was pushed up against the couch so there was space to walk.

Joe crossed the room in five steps. The kitchenette was on the right. A dinky fridge, two-burner stovetop, coffee pot and toaster oven on a counter, a sink. The bathroom was on the left. Then the bedroom. It was as big as the rest of the place put together.

Kind of nice to have some space after living in the van so long. He sat on the edge of the queen-sized bed and bounced. Softer than his mattress in the camper van. That was all right.

He opened the drapes. The window was bigger than he expected, from knee height on him nearly to the ceiling. He looked out the window. The back parking lot was deep, like somebody with a bulldozer hadn't known when to stop moving dirt. Or maybe they got paid by the yard to scrape it out and to pave it. There were two light posts, one on either side of a dumpster. The lot was bordered by patchy weeds and scraggly pine trees. Past them, hardwoods. Terry had said a nice view. Joe wasn't sure he'd go that far, but there were no buildings visible, so it was private and quiet, especially considering the busy road out front. That was what he'd asked for. This place would do for a few days. His good old gut led him straight again.

Joe moved his camper van to the back and parked it so he'd be able to see it from his window. He put his shaving kit, two pairs of pants, two shirts, two pairs of boxers in a duffel, grabbed a jacket, his red ball cap, one of the old Zane Greys he'd gotten from his dad. He slung the duffel over his shoulder and picked up the cooler with his road food. He'd get some ice later. He locked up and headed for the back door. He could move more stuff gradually, as he needed it.

The security lights came on, even though it wasn't dark yet. He checked his watch. Quarter of six. Days were getting longer. He'd mention to Terry, he ought to adjust the timer for those lights. Save some electricity.

Back upstairs, he put all his stuff away in drawers, set the duffel on a shelf in the closet, and went to close the drapes. Not that it was likely anybody could see into the room, or that anybody would try, but it seemed like the thing to do. He'd equipped the camper van windows with blinds he closed at night, and he liked the feeling of being enclosed. While he was at the window, he saw another car drive into the back lot. A late-model white Cadillac.

It stopped in a corner out of the security light's reach. The driver—a man—got out and went around to open the passenger's door for a lady. Their figures were shadowy, but what they did was clear enough. They locked lips in a kiss that made Joe squirm. The guy's hands were on her butt. They had to let go of each other at least a little to walk to the building, but Joe had the feeling they'd be naked in no time. Joe was no prude, but some people. He closed the drapes.

9

Wednesday afternoon, Lammie chatted with the client who was waiting for Attorney Morton when the telephone on her desk rang.

"Attorney Morton's office," she said.

"Hello, Lammie."

"Hello, Mr. Tatum." She struggled to keep her voice even. "How are you?"

"Fine, tending to business, thinking about you. Mostly thinking about you."

She couldn't answer.

"Do we still have a date for Friday?" he asked.

"Of course."

"I have a place for us to go, if that's OK with you. I don't want to assume too much, or pressure you, Lammie, but—"

"That will be fine, Mr. Tatum. Thank you for letting me know." She hung up and swallowed hard, grateful that her boss picked that moment to emerge from his office and greet his client.

When Lammie walked out of work that Friday afternoon, the Cadillac was idling at the curb. Cubby leaned against the hood. She felt her feet rise up off the ground, feared she'd float away, but he saw her, pushed himself away from the car, and came forward to take her hand and pull her back to earth.

He put her overnight bag in the trunk, then held the door for her to slide into the dark blue velour interior.

After that, the hours flowed, liquid as dreams.

They drove through Littleboro, took a backroad to the interstate, glided toward Raleigh, and forty-five minutes later, they landed at the Highway Home Hotel.

"I know it doesn't look like much," Cubby said when they turned into the driveway. "But it's clean, quiet, private." He drove around to the back of the building. "We're on the top floor."

"You've already checked in?"

"Earlier in the week. I've been here a few nights so I could tend to Dad's properties in Raleigh."

"How long can we stay?" she asked.

"I need to get home sometime tomorrow. But Sunday, Aunt Dru's friend Betsy is coming to stay with her for a while, so I won't have to worry about her."

Not exactly the answer she wanted—she wanted to hear him say he was hers forever from this day forward, but there was a future in what he said. That would do.

There were nice hotels downtown near the government buildings, but they would be busy, people coming and going. This was private, he said. They would be alone in a place where nobody knew them. Lammie shivered.

Cubby parked, walked around the car, and opened the door for her. He pointed to the building. "That's our room up there." Then he put his arms around her and kissed her. She held him tight, longer than he held her.

"Hang onto that feeling," he said. "I'll get your bag."

She smiled and held his arm as they crossed the parking lot and went in through a back door. The elevator was right there, waiting for them. She heard two men's voices from down a hallway but couldn't see them. That meant they couldn't see her and Cubby either. Sometimes it was good to be invisible.

Cubby held the elevator door for her, and they kissed again as it rose. When it opened on the third floor, they came face-to-face with a man waiting to go down.

Cubby touched her back, guiding her. "We're down there, honey."

Lammie ducked her head and stepped past the man. "Excuse me." When she reached the room, she looked back. Cubby still stood at the elevator, staring the man down.

"Cubby?" she called. "Is this the room?"

He turned toward her and smiled. He covered the distance between them in long strides. As soon as the room door closed behind them, she forgot everything about the world outside.

10

Joe decided to go back to the van and get his bottle of Jack Daniels. Hadn't thought of it before. Get some ice, too, while he was downstairs. He found a plastic ice bucket by the kitchenette sink, dropped his room key in his pocket, and headed out. He pressed the elevator button and realized it was already coming up from the ground floor.

The elevator door opened and there they were, the couple from the parking lot. The lady looked right at him. Pretty, with reddish-blond hair, big blue eyes. She looked down, shy. Maybe embarrassed to be here. Dressed nice in a suit like a teacher or a librarian, not like he would have expected considering what he'd seen.

She whispered, "Excuse me," stepped past him and went down the hall toward 314. Joe couldn't help himself. He turned his head and watched her walk. She was his type of woman, soft, not all angles like so many these days. Definitely not the one-night-stand type.

When Joe turned back, the man was inches from his face. Didn't say a word, just pinned Joe with a stare. The guy was younger. Taller. Broader shoulders. They stayed nose to nose for two seconds, maybe three, until Joe's feet took over and moved him back out of range.

"Cubby?" the woman called. "Is this the room?"

The guy turned and walked down the hall toward her as if Joe had disappeared.

Joe hated to admit it, but the guy had scared him for a minute. He got in the elevator and leaned against the wall while it descended. What did I do to him? he wondered. Not so scared now, more indignant, then more, what the heck?

By the time he got past the second floor, anger began to replace indignation.

By the time he got to the ice machine, he hated the guy.

Joe stewed over the encounter while he ate some beef jerky, Cheez Whiz on saltines, and seedless grapes. Supper enough. The drink helped him think of all the things he should have said to the jerk, what he'd say next time they crossed paths. What kind of name was Cubby for a grown man, anyway?

He found the old movie channel on TV and watched his dad's favorite, The African Queen, but he couldn't pay attention. His brain buzzed from the new hatred, not something he was used to feeling. It was his trusty gut, he decided, telling him to pay attention. Something wasn't right. He needed to stay awake, stay alert. Maybe that fellow Cubby had lured the pretty lady to the Highway Home. That was the only explanation for why she'd be there. Cubby was a shady guy. Somebody to keep an eye on.

Joe turned off the lights in his room and opened the drapes a few inches, enough so he could look out. If he looked straight down and to his left, he could see the sidewalk that went out from the back door, but not the door itself. His camper van held down one end of the parking lot. At the far end, the Cadillac. In between, the security lights didn't cast circles wide enough to light the whole area, so there was plenty of dark. Nothing moved in either the light or the shadows. He could close the drapes again and watch Katherine Hepburn pull leeches off Humphrey Bogart, but his gut buzzed a warning. He opened the drapes wider and dragged a chair over. No idea what he was watching for, but he'd know it when he saw it.

The movie ended and Casablanca began. He checked the clock once in a while. By quarter to eleven, the energy in his brain was ebbing. He decided to keep vigil until eleven thirty, then if nothing weird had happened, go to bed.

The Maltese Falcon had just begun when he heard a noise. He froze. The creak of a heavy door hinge. Not his door but not far away. His guess—the fire door to the stairwell, through the wall behind his bed's headboard. Somebody was going to the ground floor for ice or the vending machine. But why use the stairs, not the elevator? That was weird.

He stood up and paused, thinking, how long did it take somebody to get down the stairs? Maybe the person was going outside. He leaned the side of his head against the window to get the best view and looked down. If somebody came out the back door and took the sidewalk, he'd see them. Nothing moved. He waited some more. Still nothing. False alarm. It still felt off, though. If somebody came out and hugged the building, moving left or right, could he see them? In the morning, he'd take a closer look at the back door and get a fix on what was and wasn't visible from his window.

May as well go to bed. He moved the chair back to its place, went to the bathroom, brushed his teeth, went back to the bedroom. He stripped down to his boxers and T-shirt, folded his pants and shirt, and stacked them on the corner of the dresser. He peeled back the bedspread and top sheet.

Then he heard the creak again. Definitely the stairwell door. He checked the window one more time. There was a light out beyond the parking lot, a glow that hadn't been there before. A bright light shining up from the woods. His brain said fire, and that fast, flames shot up and grabbed for the sky.

He scrambled for the phone but there was no dial tone. Dial 0, Terry had said, so he did. After a few rings, somebody fumbled the receiver. Then, "This is Terry."

"Terry, Joe Corcoran, 312. Listen, the woods are on fire."

"What?"

"Call the fire department. The woods are burning." Joe dressed in record time, got his shoes on, and ran out of the room.

By the time Joe got outside into the back parking lot, Terry was there. He wore athletic shorts and a sweatshirt. Barefooted on the cold pavement. His long hair was a rat's nest in the back.

"Did you call 'em?" Joe asked. Then he heard a siren. Joe walked out into the parking lot, trying to see if the fire was getting close to the camper van. He should have thought to bring his keys so he could move it. Maybe he should go back for them.

He turned back toward the building and looked up. His window looked grayed out because the last thing he'd done before he ran out of the room was yank the drapes closed. But in the other window on the third floor, Room 314, the drapes were wide open. He could tell because the bare glass was hard and black with no light on inside. He knew—just knew—they were up there, Cubby and the lady, watching everything below them. Including him.

11

Cubby took charge in a way he had not when they were in her bedroom. First, he made them drinks. There was a tiny refrigerator with a tiny freezer and the smallest ice tray she'd ever seen. The ice barely cooled the bourbon he poured into the clear plastic cups. But she didn't want him to leave the room, not even to go down to the ice machine.

When he turned to her, he made her feel she was his prize, a present to be unwrapped. He liked the black lace she'd chosen to go under her business suit—she had known he would.

He wanted to look at her and posed her this way and that. In the kitchenette on the counter, on the settee, the chair. Finally, in the bed. Did she faint for a moment? She couldn't be sure.

It was hours later that Cubby lay back on the pillows. "You set my world on fire, Lammie."

And she said, "Prove it."

"Don't think I won't." He got up, pulled on his pants and shirt, shoes without socks.

"Where are you going? Don't go." She reached for him.

"Come here." He yanked the sheet off her and pulled her out of bed. Then he opened the drapes wide. "Stand here at the window. Don't turn on any lights."

Stand at a window at night, stark naked, with no curtains, no shelter from whatever was out there? She felt a twinge of panic. "Why? What are you doing?"

"Just watch." He grabbed something off the bedside table, grinned at her, and then he was gone, leaving her in the dark.

She pulled the bedspread off the bed and wrapped it around her shoulders. Whatever he was doing, wherever he was going, Cubby would not let her down. He wasn't her daddy who had died. He wasn't the senator who had lied and led her on. The fear released its hold, and she breathed.

She could not see Cubby outside in the dark, but she knew he was there. She pressed her hand and her forehead against the glass and shivered. Moments went by. Something glimmered at the edge of her vision, faltered, then caught like a slow-building flame. It was a flame. And another. Blue and yellow and scarlet. Tiny fiery birds flew upward, outward. They found perches, lit up those perches, and made more flames.

She gasped. He had set the world on fire. For her.

She heard the room door open, dropped the bedspread, and ran to meet him.

"Call 911," he said. "Hurry."

"What?"

"Here." He picked up the phone beside the bed and dialed the number himself. Then he handed her the receiver. "Tell them there's a fire in the woods behind the Highway Home Hotel."

What was happening? Lammie could barely speak when the 911 operator answered. "There's a fire. In the woods. Highway Home Hotel."

"Tell them to hurry," Cubby whispered.

"Hurry," Lammie said. The operator began to ask a question, but Cubby took the phone and hung up.

He grinned at her and shed his clothes. "Let's watch the show." He picked up the bedspread from the floor, draped it around both of them, and slid his arm around her waist.

They stood together at the window, the room dark behind them, and watched. Fire walked crazily along the ground. Tree limbs glowed and burned. It all looked the way she'd felt when Cubby made love to her.

Then sirens. Fire trucks filled the parking lot. Lights, noise, thick hoses, men in bulky suits moving as if through deep mud. And in moments, the flames were gone.

Lammie sighed and leaned into him. "I didn't want it to end. Why did you make the call so soon?"

He nuzzled her neck. "Fire can get out of control. We don't want anybody to get hurt."

And then they fell onto the bed.

In the wee hours, Lammie lay awake, curled behind him,

spooned around him. She felt his ribs rise and fall. He snored a little, twitched, resettled. It suited her not to sleep, to absorb every moment of their togetherness, so long in coming. She could touch the freckles on the back of his neck as much as she wanted. They sparked when she touched them, singed her fingers.

12

Maureen Boykin left her small gray house at seven thirty that Friday morning. It was March 26, her birthday, but there was no boss to tell her to take the day off. She'd gotten a last-minute call to investigate a fire on a farm northeast of Raleigh, and freelancers never turned down work.

She slung a tote bag over her shoulder and carried a duffel in each hand to her Wagoneer. It was heavy, all the stuff she carried to every scene, not knowing what she'd need until she got there. The part of the state she was headed for, what people called East, was big, low-lying, and sparsely populated. She couldn't count on handy gas stations where she could ask directions—she hated to ask directions anyway—so she laid a roadmap on the passenger's seat, her route marked with broad yellow highlighter. She taped a note card with road numbers and turns in large print to the dashboard where she could sneak quick glances. She took a deep breath, started the car, and backed it out of the driveway.

The fire chief in a small farming community had called her to take a look at a barn that had burned. It went up fast, he said. In Maureen's experience, barns did that. Lots of flammable stuff.

The chief said something about hogs, so she'd asked if there were any animals in the barn when it burned. She didn't deal with dead animals or humans. No, the chief said, property damage only.

Still, figuring out the source and cause was beyond the volunteer firefighters' abilities. The insurance company was going to send its own investigator, but not for a couple of weeks, and that person would be taking care of the company's interests. Maureen's neck tingled a little. Did that mean the insurance company would be looking for signs the owner burned his own property? Did they know something she didn't?

As the chief talked, he disclosed that the farmer who owned the barn happened to be his cousin. And all they wanted was an objective finding. In Maureen's experience, an objective finding meant not giving the insurance company an excuse not to pay. She sometimes worked for insurance companies, so she hoped the cause of this fire would be clear and simple. She didn't want to wrangle with a potential bigger client.

Maureen was good at navigating and arrived right when she said she would, nine thirty. The dirt farm road she turned onto was long and straight. Fields on either side had been tilled for spring planting. She didn't know much about farming, but the place looked prosperous to her. They probably had a tobacco allotment to go with the hog operation.

The farmer, his wife, their two adult sons, and the fire chief-cousin were gathered to greet her at the end of the road. Two young boys, maybe ten and twelve years old, hovered behind the grownups.

Maureen introduced herself, shook hands all around, then the farmer and the fire chief walked her around a big two-story white house with a wrap-around porch. Behind it, one hundred feet away, she saw the barn, a blackened wooden structure that had collapsed into itself. Small footprint, not a big building. The long, low pig parlors and big metal barns were well away from it and the house.

It struck her odd that plastic stanchions stood at the four corners of the burned-out barn and crime scene tape was draped around them. In Maureen's mind, it wasn't a crime scene until she said it was. And wasn't she supposed to find it wasn't an arson fire, that the farmer hadn't struck the match? It was all a little confusing.

Maureen listened while the farmer described coming out of the back door, seeing the smoke, running back inside to call 911, then grabbing the kitchen fire extinguisher. About that time, the barn exploded.

While she listened, Maureen looked around. Sheets of tin roofing had been thrown around the yard. Smaller, heavier metal fragments lay in the grass like unmelting hailstones. Charred beams had blown outward.

"What did you keep in the barn?"

"An old tractor that was my dad's. I kept it running, more like a hobby than to use it. I give the grandkids rides sometimes. I would have taught them to drive it when they got tall enough." He pointed to the two boys who had followed them, not coming close, but there. They turned away from their grandfather's attention.

A tractor with a gas tank—no wonder the building blew up.

"What else was in it?" she asked.

"I had a little work bench, some hand tools. My wife had some stuff for her flower beds."

"Stuff like fertilizer? Bags of mulch?"

"I guess so."

"The fire could have been a lot worse, then. You're lucky it didn't spread." Maureen opened her car's back hatch and pulled the duffels out.

"That's the truth."

"Yeah," the chief said, "but fire on a farm. We can't be casual about that."

Maureen hung her camera around her neck. "I'm never casual about fire."

There was a stand of tall pine trees off to one side, and motion from that direction caught her eye. Three men she took to be farmworkers—overalls, canvas jackets, boots—were watching, but like the kids, keeping their distance.

She stepped over the tape and got to work.

When she'd finished, Maureen gestured for the fire chief to come talk to her apart from the family. "The owner knows insurance doesn't cover arson, right?"

"He does, yeah." The man looked over his shoulder, then shifted so no one could see his face except Maureen. "We're not talking about anything of value here, though. We just want to be sure the right thing gets done." His head twitched in the direction of the pine trees, the direction of the three men.

She picked up the vibe. The farmer believed the fire was deliberately set. Those three workmen? Maybe they'd had a run-in with the boss. Substandard housing, long hours, light scales, slow clocks. If the farmer thought the men did it, he wanted them in trouble more than he wanted a settlement for an old barn and tractor, and he wanted it fast. Faster than the insurance company adjuster would get there. Objective, like the chief had said. Someone with no dog in the fight.

Maureen kept herself from turning toward the three men again. Focused on the chief. "I'm not sure why you bothered to call me then." Not true, but what would he say?

He shrugged again. All she had to say was arson and those workers were toast. No pun intended. Under her coveralls, her hackles rose.

"I need to get out of this gear and make notes about my findings." She headed for her car.

The chief walked back toward the farmer. The two boys kicked and stomped chunks of ashy wood that lay outside the taped perimeter.

Maureen didn't lie about wanting to get out of her coveralls. They were hot, no matter what the weather, and it was warm for March. She had sweat running down her back and legs. She needed water and a Snickers bar.

But the farmer and fire chief were antsy. They gave her five minutes before they were beside her.

"What are you thinking?" the chief asked.

"I don't deliver my reports on the spot," she said.

"But it wasn't an accident," the farmer said. He wasn't asking.

"Sir, I've learned not to do guesswork. It's too easy to get tunnel vision."

"Yeah, but you're working for us—"

She looked to the chief. "Maybe I should have said up front, I may be freelance, but that doesn't mean I'm a hired gun."

He put a hand on the farmer's shoulder. "Come on, Big Tom. Let's let the lady do her job."

Lady. She tore open the candy wrapper with her teeth and ate half the bar in one bite. Farmer Big Tom wanted to argue, but he let his cousin steer him away.

The two boys had gravitated to their grandfather and his cousin. They dawdled. She raised a hand. "Hi. No school today?"

"No, ma'am," one of them said.

"Want a Snickers?"

Sure they did. She asked a few questions while they ate. The younger one was the talker. She found out they liked to fish and ride dirt bikes around the farm. They liked weekends at the family beach cottage.

"How did it happen?" she asked. "The fire."

And it all came out. They were sneaking a cigarette they'd stolen out of the box Granddad kept on the back porch because Grandma wouldn't let him smoke inside anymore.

There it was. The reason the farmer had stepped out onto the back porch just as the barn went up. He wanted a smoke.

"Are we in trouble?" the older boy asked. "I mean, jail?"

"No, not jail, but your granddad will probably make you pay for the rest of your lives. Come on. You have to tell them right now. It'll only get worse. And let me tell you, fire is nothing to fool around with. You have to know, you were lucky."

"Yes, ma'am," in unison.

The older boy was still nervous. Had he been canny enough to try and cast blame in another direction? Could he have said something to Granddad about the workers? Maureen sighed. She couldn't make that her problem.

The fire chief insisted on taking her to a late lunch at the county's best barbecue joint. The local sheriff—who turned out to be another cousin—joined them so Maureen could tell him about the fire. When the sheriff heard the story, he rumbled about teaching the kids a lesson, then about how the farmer was well-respected in the county, a big supporter of all the charities—Maureen guessed by charity he meant his re-election campaign—so he'd just have a serious talk with Big Tom and the boys' parents and keep a close eye on them from then on.

"OK, I just don't want to be back down here investigating another fire," she said.

Maureen sat in her car making a few last notes and waiting for the men to leave. She was two hours from home, an hour from the coast. She decided the ocean and a seafood dinner would be worth the detour. A woman didn't turn forty-one every day.

The beach access parking lot was deserted, and so was the beach. Wind off the ocean was chilly and too stiff to walk in, so she sat on a set of steps that took people over the dunes and watched shore birds for a while. She felt good about the results of her work that day, and it was good to let her mind empty out.

She got a table by the window looking out over slow silver-gray waves. One margarita sipped slow and cushioned by a plate of fried oysters and shrimp, hushpuppies, slaw, and a slice of Key lime pie, wouldn't hurt her or her driving skills. She had enough Motown and classic country on the tape deck to get her home.

13

It was ten thirty when Maureen pulled into the driveway of her little gray house. She hadn't expected to be so late getting back, but still, she ought to have left the porch light on.

Her neighborhood was quiet, and people looked out for each other, but the younger ones were out somewhere on Friday night, the older ones in bed or thinking about it. No one saw her struggle into the dark house with her duffels and tote. Heavier now than when she'd left that morning. It had been a long day, but all in all, not bad. She'd done something right and got to have her own little celebration.

Maureen left her stuff inside the front door and collapsed on the couch. She would rest a few minutes then unpack and shower before bed.

When she roused herself and checked her watch, she found she'd been asleep almost an hour. Unpacking could wait until morning. She got up, wandered toward her bedroom, undressing as she went. The telephone rang. That meant going into the kitchen where the table doubled as her desk. Her office. She got the phone on the fourth ring.

"Maureen Boykin," she said.

"Hey, Maureen. Sorry to wake you. It's J.J. Ralston."

"Hey, J.J. What's up?"

Ralston was a captain in the Raleigh fire department. She'd known him for a while and knew he didn't call to check on her well-being.

"We had a spark of some kind get loose in the woods behind the Highway Home Hotel on South Road. You know it?"

"I've driven by."

"It didn't amount to much, but I'd like you to check it out for the department. I can authorize your usual fee, no problem."

That meant her fee was less than the overtime he'd have to pay one of his own people. Not to mention the ill will of a call this late on a Friday night. Ill will was a luxury Maureen couldn't afford.

"Tonight?" She shook off the fatigue. These odd jobs were her bread and butter. And if it was nothing much, all the better.

"Meet you there. How do you take your coffee?"

"Better make it black, this time of night."

What was it about her birthday the universe didn't understand?

A fire truck pulled out of the hotel's driveway as Maureen pulled in. She drove around to the back and saw a second fire truck, its crew stowing equipment, getting ready to leave. A Cadillac was parked in the near corner of the lot and an old VW camper van on the far side. There was a dumpster in between the two, a light pole on either side of the dumpster. J.J. was in the middle of it all, standing next to his Suburban with the Raleigh Fire Department emblem and talking into his radio. Maureen stopped beside him.

He ended his call. "Thanks for coming out, Maureen." He handed her an insulated mug and poured coffee from a plaid thermos.

If the day had felt like spring, the night reminded her, they weren't far removed from winter. She needed the coffee for the jolt and the warmth.

"What have we got?" she asked.

"Not much more than a brush fire," he said. "There's a homeless camp about half a mile through the woods. The hotel manager says some of them wander over once in a while, asking about work or whatever. It could have been one of them out for a stroll, maybe dropped a cigarette."

"Where was the fire?" Maureen asked. It wasn't visible in the circles the security lights cast.

"See where the Cadillac is parked? It's between there and the dumpster. A good twenty feet back. Some scrubby pines got involved, but another twenty feet from there, you're into hardwoods, so it's a good thing we got here quick."

Maureen guessed the hardwoods had once occupied all the space the hotel took. They had been cleared, pushed back for construction, and now the young pines J.J. pointed out had grown up in the gap between parking lot and woods.

Maureen heard a man's voice call out from behind them. "Hey, hey."

"Ugh," J.J. said. "This guy."

A man jogged across the parking lot, coming toward them. "Captain, is this the investigator? Did you tell her?"

"This is Mr. Corcoran," J.J. said. "He's staying in the hotel, up there on the third floor." J.J. nodded upward toward the building. "He says he didn't see anything having to do with the fire."

"Maybe I didn't see, but that doesn't mean I don't know." Mr. Corcoran puffed his chest out.

Maureen judged him to be late forties. He was at least three inches shorter than J.J., and she saw him stretch his neck as best he could to gain a little height. Corcoran looked pale, even allowing for the bad light. He wore a red ball cap pulled low, the way men without much hair often did. He didn't have a big frame. His open jacket over a T-shirt showed a soft midsection. Not an outdoorsy guy, then.

"Maureen Boykin. Fire investigator." She held out her hand. "Can I help you, Mr. Corcoran?" She glanced at J.J., who looked at his watch. Relax, she thought, I don't charge you by the hour.

"Call me Joe." He shook hands. "I told the captain here. I was in my room. 312. Good view of all this." His gesture took in the parking lot, the woods. "I stayed awake late because the guy who drives the Caddy, he gave me this bad feeling. You ever get a feeling about things, like you know something's going to happen?"

He looked at her like he expected an answer. She nodded, then shook her head. Let him take it as he wanted to.

"And I was right." Joe pointed toward the woods with his chin. "Something did. When I looked out and saw the flames, I grabbed the phone. No dial tone. So I dialed 0 to get the desk, told Terry to call 911."

"Lucky you looked out," Maureen said. Was she supposed to know who Terry was?

"Like I said, I'd been watching."

"Did you see anything besides the flames?"

"If by see, you mean with my eyes, I would have to say no. But it was the man from 314." He pointed to the third-floor window on the far corner. "He did it."

"I need to talk to my guys over there," J.J. said. "You OK, Maureen?" He didn't wait for her to answer.

So J.J. didn't think much of Joe Corcoran's story. Maureen looked back to Joe. He'd probably been a good little boy—eager to please, eager to get a gold star—and still was. She thought about the boys at the farm. That wasn't the first time she'd sussed out who lit a match, going on nothing but a tingle in her spine. A feeling, like Joe said.

"I can't do much till daylight," she said. "I'm going to take a look at the burn site, then rope it off. I'll be back in the morning. Can I talk to you then?"

"I'll be here," he said. "And I plan to be on the lookout all night."

"Good to know."

She went to her car to get her gear. Joe walked past her, and when she glanced at him, he gave her a thumbs-up.

J.J. joined her and they watched Joe disappear inside.

"Attention-seeker," J.J. said. "There's always one, right?"

She opened the trunk of her car and leaned in.

"And let's not forget," J.J. said, "he is one of the ones who called it in."

"He said somebody named Terry made the call."

"Yeah, the manager, desk clerk, whatever. But it was Joe who told him to. Dispatch got a second call, too, almost the same time as the first. A woman, but she didn't stay on the line, so we don't know who it was."

"Another person staying here?" She looked up at the window Joe had pointed to, the one he said was 314. It was a flat, black space. That meant the drapes were open and the lights were out. Somebody up there could be watching now, knowing they couldn't be seen. Creepy.

"Stands to reason," J.J. said.

"Then you've got Joe, the mystery caller, and maybe some homeless guy as possible suspects?" Not my job, she reminded herself, but the day had come full circle. She began to pull on her coveralls. They felt like they were made of lead. "I need twenty minutes. Get your guys in the truck to shine their headlights over the burn for me?"

The headlights from the fire truck showed her a swath of ground drenched from the hoses. They had wet down an area a lot bigger than the fire's locus. Firefighters' boots had stomped it to mud, but their steps stopped at the edge of the charred dirt. Maureen stopped where they had and leaned over to study the spot where the fire started.

Whoever did it had bothered to set the fire close to a big pile of rocks and had even pulled a few out to make a rough circle, as if for a campfire. Would a homeless person have done that? Why, if there was an encampment through the woods?

She backed away, drove a few yellow plastic stakes into the ground, and wound them with tape. It wouldn't keep anybody out, but who was going to come looking? If there had been property damage, any threat to people, she could have asked for a cop to protect it overnight, but no need. Another forty-five minutes at the scene in the morning, and her report would write itself. If she stuck to her business. No questions, no tingles.

Before she got back in her car, she looked at the third-floor windows again. This time, the window on the right was a blur. Whoever had been up there watching had drawn the drapes. The window on the left must be Joe's. She saw a seam of light from top to bottom, down the middle. He'd promised to keep an eye on things. A man of his word, then.

An hour later, she was home again. This time, she'd left lights on. She was too tired to turn them off, just headed for bed.

Joe watched Maureen Boykin from his window. He'd been skeptical about a woman being an investigator, especially one on the scrawny side and who, from the looks of her, didn't even own a hair curler. But she seemed to know her business. She said she'd be back in the morning and would talk to him again then. Good.

In a while, she packed up and left. The last fire truck left. The captain drove off. Joe dozed in the chair by the window. Woke with a stiff neck. Checked to be sure the Cadillac was still there. The sky was beginning to lighten. He took off his shoes, undressed, crawled under the covers.

14

Lammie woke, blinked, and sighed back into the pillows. She opened her eyes again and realized she was alone in bed. She sat up. Water was running somewhere. The shower. He was in the shower. She stretched, surprised to find her muscles were stiff when they had been so fluid a few hours earlier.

The water flow stopped. She put her feet on the floor and took a breath before she stood up. Her black lace slip lay at her feet. She lifted it and slid it over her head. She glanced in the mirror and saw her hair—tangled, unruly. She tried to smooth it and heard the bathroom door open. Cubby appeared, a towel around his waist. His short hair was spiked from being roughly dried. His cheeks were shaved so smooth, they glowed. His chest and arms were reddened from hot water.

"Hey," he said. "Sleep well?" He walked straight to her,

put his hands on her hips, looked into her eyes. "You are so beautiful."

She leaned into him to keep from saying, I'm not. I'm not beautiful. She wanted him to think that as long as possible. She thought he might want to make love again, but he held her lightly. It wasn't urgent, as all their embraces had been up until then. It was easy instead. Comfortable.

"You hungry?" he asked. "I am."

"We never ate anything, did we?"

"Food never crossed my mind."

She pressed her face into his chest again.

"What?" he said. "Are you shy in the mornings?"

"Maybe." She gave him a little shove. "At least until I wash my face."

"Why don't I go down and ask the guy at the desk if there's a breakfast place around here?"

"What time is it?"

"Going on ten." He released her and began to gather his clothes. She slipped into the bathroom and waited to use the toilet until she heard him go out. Silly. Like the man didn't know women pee. But when had she shared a bathroom with anybody other than Mama?

She brushed her teeth, showered, dampening her hair just enough to get it in order. She put on a set of daytime underwear—white cotton, eyelet trimmed—her dark blue skirt from the suit she wore to work the day before, and a fresh white vee-neck sweater. She was putting on lipstick when Cubby let himself back in.

"It's me," he called.

She met him in the sitting room. "Oh. Did we do that?" The cushions from the couch were tossed on the floor. The chairs had been moved around.

"Yes, ma'am."

She began to straighten things.

"Afraid of what the cleaning lady will think?" He laughed, then picked up a couch cushion. "Terry, the desk guy, told me about a diner not far from here. He wanted to talk about the fire, or I'd have been back sooner. Most excitement he's had in a while, I guess."

"What did he say?"

"He wanted to know if the sirens bothered us. I said we were sound asleep and missed the whole thing."

"Did he believe that?"

"He said, 'I knew that Joe was crazy,' or something like that." He put the last cushion back on the couch and thumped it into place.

"Who's Joe?"

"No clue. You ready?"

When he opened the door, Lammie heard the sound of a vacuum cleaner down the hallway. She was glad they'd straightened up.

Cubby carried her bag. They rode down in the elevator, went out the back door, and crossed the parking lot. The burned area was marked off with stakes and yellow tape—a splotch of blackened ground, a few skinny pine branches, scorched and pitiful.

The flames—remembering them lit up Lammie's nerves all over again. But she remembered another night, too, when she stood at a window, a scared little girl. Lights and sirens in the dark, people yelling, running. Maybe last night's flames had burned those memories, left them like this patch of ruined ground. Maybe Cubby had burned them for her, replaced them with something good.

"Lammie?" he called. "Let's go." The car was running.

She got in and slid across the seat to sit close. "Are we going to do it again?"

"Do what?" He gave her a wide-eyed, teasing grin and put the car in reverse.

"Are we going to set the world on fire again?" She punched his arm. "What did you think I meant?"

"No more fires for me. You're enough."

It was late for breakfast, early for lunch, so the diner was mostly empty. The waitress poured coffee without asking. Cubby didn't open the menu. He ordered orange juice, pancakes, eggs, grits, biscuits, bacon, sausage.

"Just bring it," he told the waitress. "We'll divvy it up."

Lammie held her mug in both hands and watched him. The waitress liked Cubby's looks, wanted to flirt, Lammie could tell. She didn't mind. It made her feel proud. Besides, he didn't give the girl a second look. His eyes were on Lammie the whole time.

Now she could look at him across the table, extend a foot and touch his leg—it was all so new. When he smiled, dams broke inside her.

"What are you thinking?" he asked.

"I'm not thinking. I may never think again."

"I look at your angel face, and I know your brain is going ninety miles an hour."

"OK." She lowered the mug to the table. "I was thinking, can I set the next fire?"

He held a finger to his lips. "Don't say that out loud. Arson is a crime."

"Is it?" She opened her eyes wide, teasing.

"I mean it, Lammie. I got a little crazy last night. I've burned enough stuff in my life. It isn't going to happen again."

"What do you mean, you've burned enough?"

He shook his head. "I'll tell you later, not here."

More secrets, and he was going to tell her. He was going to trust her again.

"I've got a secret too," she said. "My own crime."

"You? You've probably never gotten a speeding ticket."

She held his gaze while the waitress slid plates and platters onto the table.

When they were alone again, Lammie whispered, "I steal money."

Cubby had two pancakes on a fork, moving them from the platter to her plate. His hand froze. "I can't tell if you're serious."

She let the pause stand.

"You're serious?" he said. "You are serious." He put the fork down. "What money?"

"Filing fees," she said. "I tell clients they have to pay filing fees in cash—that's true—and then I just say a five-dollar fee is ten, a ten-dollar fee is fifteen." She took a slice of toast and a scoop of scrambled eggs. "I keep the extra."

"Damn, Lammie. How long has this been going on?"

"Years now. Almost since I started working for Attorney Morton. The first time was an honest mistake. I went to the courthouse to file some papers and realized I'd charged the client too much. It was the end of the day, so I thought, I'll fix it tomorrow. Then overnight, I figured out, nobody knew. Nobody would ask. And nobody ever has."

"Morton doesn't know?"

"Him?" She snorted. "He's too busy being a big shot. He's happy not to be bothered. He says that's what he has me for. And the clients? They say they don't know what they'd do without me."

"But why take the risk?"

"Everybody else takes what they want. Why shouldn't I?"

His eyes were more brown than green, darker than usual. And puzzled. "It can't be much money, those little bits and pieces." He sounded like he was trying to convince himself.

"You'd be surprised how it adds up."

"Y'all need a warm-up?" The waitress had a coffee pot in her hand.

"Yes, please," Lammie said. "It's good. What brand do y'all use?"

She didn't listen to the answer, just studied Cubby's face. What was he thinking about her confession?

They finished eating without saying much more. He left a twenty-dollar bill on the table.

The traffic lights were green between the diner and the interstate. Cubby drove like it was a job that demanded all of his attention, even though traffic was light. He's mulling, she thought, taking it in. She smiled and ran her hand over the plush upholstery. She liked riding in the Cadillac.

Cubby broke the silence. "Have you ever noticed, Littleboro isn't even mentioned on the exit signs? If you didn't know it was there, you couldn't find our hometown."

"No wonder nobody new ever shows up."

"Just bad pennies like me." He paused at the stop sign at the bottom of the exit ramp and looked at her.

She slid across the seat and kissed him. "You're the good penny. The big handsome shiny penny."

There was one gas station at their exit. Cubby pulled in but drove past the pumps and stopped at the edge of its parking lot. He killed the engine and shifted to face her. "I still don't understand about the money."

"Are you upset with me?" Had she misjudged him? The car began to cool. Or was the chill something else?

"Not upset. I just want to understand."

She'd have to tell him all of it, or more than she'd planned. "It goes way back. After Daddy got shot, Mama sent me to stay with his parents for a while, on their farm. I missed my daddy so much, and so did they. I didn't want to go, but after a little while, I wanted to stay with them forever. Then Mama came to get me right before Christmas, and they said she needed me.

"The day before I left, Granny took me down to the cellar and showed me an old coffee can she had hidden there. It had money in it. She said I should remember, a woman needs some money of her own, and that when she died, I should take the coffee can and not tell anybody. I asked her where the money came from, and she said a smart woman knows how to tuck a little away."

"Did she die?"

"She was already sick then, but they didn't want to tell me. She died less than a year later. When Mama took me to the funeral, I did what Granny told me to do. I sneaked down into the cellar and found her money. I still have it, every dollar, hidden away. Thirty-four dollars and sixty-seven cents."

"You think your granny would be happy with you?"

"I've done what she told me to do."

He turned to look out the windshield. Lammie did the same. Her mouth was dry. When he began to talk, his words were slow.

"When I was a kid, my dad burned trash in a metal drum. That's what people did then."

"I remember."

"I liked the flames when they first flared up. When nobody was watching, I put extra stuff in, stuff that burned hot, just to get the flames. By the time I was a teenager, it was my regular chore. I felt good when I did it. Fire relaxed me when things were bad with Dad."

He was bringing those words up from a deep well, she knew.

"I didn't set fire to anything but trash until I was in the army. Then, I got trained to work with explosives. It was legit. Anytime I was bored or stressed, I could make something burn. Flames were my medicine."

Medicine. Like her Friday afternoons after work when she went into her secret room, added the week's money to a shoebox, recorded the new total in her notebook. Her medicine. Except for yesterday, when Cubby had picked her up. She had forty dollars in her purse to add as soon as she could.

"But Vietnam—what I saw there—I hated what my work did. What burned because of me. It made me sick." He closed his eyes and shook his head. "I got it out of my system. The fire last night—it may have been a crazy show-off thing to do, but it wasn't careless. I made a circle of rocks. No chance of the fire spreading, no chance of anybody getting hurt. But like I said, I'm never going to do it again."

"Because you don't need to," she said. "I'm your medicine now."

He took her hand and kissed it. "And we're two people who keep secrets—but not from each other, right?"

15

"Where have you been?"

Maureen had barely gotten out of her car when she heard the voice. She turned around and saw Joe Corcoran hustling across the hotel parking lot toward her. He wore baggy tan pants, a navy blue windbreaker half zipped over a plaid shirt, and the same red ball cap.

He stopped his roll a few feet in front of her. "I thought you'd be here a couple of hours ago. You missed them."

Was this guy always a pain in the rear? "Missed who?"

"That Cubby and the pretty lady. You want to interview them, right?" He pointed at a dark window on the backside of the hotel—the one she'd thought somebody watched from the night before—then to the corner of the parking lot. It was empty, but she remembered there'd been a car there, a Cadillac, she thought.

She wasn't sure who he meant by Cubby and the pretty lady but had a safe answer. "I don't interview people." She opened her trunk and pulled out her gear.

"But he did it."

Without looking at him, she could tell Joe was shifting from foot to foot, not going away. She stepped into coveralls and snapped them up.

"Mr. Corcoran." She looked him in the eye. "It's not my job to do interviews or determine who did what. I look at the burn site. I analyze it. I tell the authorities—police, fire, insurance—what I find. They take it from there."

"But arson." He flung his hands up, his fingers making explosions in the air.

"If it was. I can't say that until I do my job."

"And then?"

"I pack up. I go to my office." He didn't need to know her office was her kitchen table. "I write my report. I send it in. I go to the next job. So, if you'll excuse me." She reached for shoe covers.

"All right." He took a few steps back. "But what if nobody does anything about him, and he's some crazy firebug? What if he does it again? Whose fault will that be?"

"Not yours. Not mine."

"Yeah, well." He didn't move. "You're saying you don't get involved. But that's not how I do things."

She pushed down the thought that he could be right. A senseless act of arson, burning nothing, doing no damage except to some weedy pine trees—it was easy to dismiss, but that kind of fire was about one thing. The fire itself. People who liked fire were going to light fires, and they weren't always so harmless.

She remembered what Captain Ralston had said about Joe Corcoran. Attention-seeker. The one who called it in. She grasped what the captain had left unsaid, hanging in the air for her. Joe himself might be the crazy firebug, needing to get a little excitement into his life. It was an often-told war story among fire fighters.

"How well do you know this guy, Cubby?" And, she didn't say out loud, why are you trying to pin the fire on him?

Joe swayed back on his heels, then shrugged. "I don't know him, exactly. I had a little run-in with him right after they got here, him and the lady. I didn't do a thing, and he was in my face. That's when I knew he wasn't right."

Joe irritating somebody by not doing a thing? Imagine that. "And?"

"I heard her, his lady friend, call him Cubby. But I checked with Terry the desk clerk and his real name is Quinn Tatum. He comes from a little town not far away. Now why does a guy who lives less than an hour from here rent a hotel room for a month? Huh?"

"I can think of lots of reasons. What's your best guess?"

Now Joe looked at the ground and screwed his lips from frown to grimace. Maureen could tell, he didn't want to say sex, but that's what he was thinking.

"She's a pretty lady," he said. "Doesn't look like the type."

Maureen translated to herself: Cubby was younger, taller, better looking than poor old Joe. "Well, I guess we agree about why they were here. How about you, Mr. Corcoran? Why are you here?"

It was a magic question. He lit up like a Christmas tree. "I'm a free man. I live in my camper van, and nobody tells me what to do, where to go. And I look for chances to help folks on the road. That's my calling in life. Helping."

And that's what he thought he was doing now. Helping. Or had he created the chance to help? J.J.'s grumble came back to her.

"Is that your van?" Maureen looked past him to study it. "It's seen some miles, I guess."

It was painted a muddy tan on top and a khaki green on the bottom, both dulled by time, weather, and road wear. There were a few dings and a deep scratch on the driver's side, facing Maureen.

"May not look like much, but I take good care of the insides. That's why I'm here to stay a few days. Monday morning, I'm going to find a good mechanic, get a tune-up, oil change, new filters. Tires too. You want to see inside?"

"Sure." To her surprise, she did want to see.

He trotted around to the passenger side, and she followed. He unlocked and slid the door back. She leaned in. Maybe she expected drifts of fast-food wrappers, empty Coke cans, general debris, and the smell of old French fries, but the carpeted floor was clean, the dashboard shiny, the vinyl seats gleamed. The van had a lemony aroma. There were only two seats, the driver's and front passenger's. Behind them, built-in cabinets ran front to back and top to bottom along the sides, their doors all closed and latched. A narrow platform bed stretched across the far end. The blanket covering it was tucked in tight.

"Nice," Maureen said. "Did you build it out?"

"I did. I made it to suit me."

"That's rare in life, to be able to suit yourself."

"I feel pretty sorry for anybody who can't do that."

"Then you feel sorry for most of us, don't you?" She stepped back. "You don't need to work for a living?"

"I have some money. Enough for me. No taxes. It's the taxes that keep people living hand to mouth." He took another look around the interior, as if her presence could have caused things to shift, then slid the door shut and locked it.

"You never miss having a life in one place? Friends? A favorite place to eat?" Maureen asked.

"What I have is better. For me at least."

He was probably right.

"Thanks for the tour," Maureen said. "I'd better get to work, or the whole day will be gone." She walked back to her car for her camera bag and notebook.

"You don't believe me, do you? About Cubby and the fire." Joe sounded sad now. "I felt like you might be the one to listen."

Maureen felt the tingle, the urge to know, and took time to shove it down. She was on good terms with J.J. Ralston, appreciated the work that came her way even if it was the odd late-night no-big-deal cases like this one. But it was her nature to resist other people's agendas. Like Farmer Big Tom and his cousins, thinking they could use her to make their case against his workers. J.J. had been looking for an easy answer. A homeless person or Joe. No need to look any further.

Whoever did it, that wasn't Maureen's job, but she had the tingle, the curiosity, and the idea of the firebug who'd do it again. Was Joe predicting? Or was he confessing? Was prediction a confession?

This was crazy thinking.

"Let me say this, Joe. It sounds as if you don't like this guy Cubby for whatever reason, and it's easy to think bad about somebody you don't like. But you said you didn't see him or anybody out here before you saw the fire. Maybe my investigation will turn something up, but in my experience, in a case like this, if there's been no harm done, nobody is going to care."

"You saw this place last night. The lighting out here, it's

bad. It wouldn't be hard to slip from shadow to shadow—"

Uh-oh. He was getting revved up. She needed to put a stop to it. "I get that, but that's not enough to go on."

"Not enough for the cops and the fire chief. They're going to be stuck because they want evidence. I could lie and say I saw something besides those shadows, but I don't tell lies. People like you and me—we're not stuck like they are. We don't have to see something to know it's real."

What made him believe that about her? The night before, he'd asked her if she ever got a feeling about something, but it wasn't a real question. He had been telling her he knew she did. Get feelings, get tingles. And now he was pulling her into his version of what had happened.

"I need to get to work."

Joe looked like somebody had stuck a thumb in his bowl of ice cream.

Maureen approached the fire site with her camera and took photos of the book she'd seen the night before—it turned out to be a Raleigh phone book—and the paper towel in situ. She decided not to collect them because if anybody wanted to pursue the arson thing, they could be evidence, and that meant they belonged to the police. Some small branches and woodsy debris had been added to the fire. The tree line was close enough that whoever set the fire didn't have to go far for material. It showed intent, but probably not a long-planned intention. There was no smell of gas but plenty of accelerants left no odor. Somebody had probably dowsed the phone book and a bunch of the towels and struck a match. She doubted she'd get far trying to figure out what was used. She wouldn't speculate either.

The whole time she worked, she could feel Joe Corcoran's eyes on her from the upstairs window. Those windows—was saomebody always up there on the third floor looking out? It didn't seem as creepy in the daylight as it had the night before.

When she headed back to her car, she waved up to Joe's window. She stowed her camera, took off her overalls and boot protectors, and sat in the car to make a few notes. She would drop the film at a camera shop where they would develop it for her quickly. Then she decided she ought to find a lady's room before making the drive across town.

Maureen went inside the hotel and followed a hallway that looked like it would go to the lobby. The registration desk was ahead and to her left. A skinny young guy stood there, studying a magazine open on the counter in front of him. He looked up.

"Hey," he said. "I saw you out there."

"You must be Terry."

"Yes, ma'am." He straightened and grinned.

"I'd like to get your account of the fire, if you don't mind." He wouldn't know it wasn't her job.

"Sure." He was as eager as Joe to talk. "I was sound asleep in my apartment when Mr. Corcoran called." He pointed backwards with his thumb. "I looked out my window and saw the flames, so I dialed 911. Soon as I got off the phone, I grabbed a fire extinguisher and went outside. We're close to a firehouse, so I heard sirens right away."

"And you didn't see anybody around?"

"Not except for Mr. Corcoran. Joe."

"I hear there was one other room occupied on the third floor at the back."

"That's right." Terry nodded. "A Mr. Tatum from right

down the road in Littleboro."

"But you didn't see him at all during the fire?"

"No, ma'am. He took the room a few days ago, comes and goes. I didn't even know he was here last night until Joe told me."

She asked a few more questions—not her business, but since Terry liked to talk, why not? It was the first time Quinn Tatum had been a guest at the Highway Home. He'd checked in on Tuesday—Terry checked his records to get the day right—and he'd taken the extended stay rate. Last night, he must have used the back door when he came in, maybe while Terry took his supper break.

"So, you are taking Joe's word for it?" She loaded the question with skepticism. How good was Joe's word for anything? Terry blinked. Maureen saw the wheels turning.

"Joe told me later, he had a lady friend with him," Terry said. "I guess that's why he was low key about it. Then this morning he came down and asked me where they could get a good breakfast. We, he said, like more than just him."

"You didn't see the lady yourself?"

He scrunched his face, figuring it out. "No, but I guess that's why a man who lives so close needs a room here."

"That would explain it," Maureen said, and Terry blushed. Then she remembered why she'd come into the hotel in the first place. "Is there a restroom I can use?"

"The cleaning ladies have one in their break room, right back down that hall, the door with the Staff Only sign on it. Tell them I said it was OK."

"Thanks, Terry."

She had missed seeing the small door when she came in, but there it was, across the hall from the elevator and snack machines. She knocked and somebody called, "Just a minute."

A young woman opened the door. She wore a floral-printed smock over a black turtleneck and blue jeans. Her blond hair was skinned back into a ponytail not unlike Maureen's. "Did you need something, ma'am?"

"Hi. I'm here investigating the fire from last night. Terry said I might be able to use the ladies room."

"Oh sure, come on in." The woman opened the door wider. Maureen stepped into a small room crowded with furniture too big for it.

A second woman—same age, same clothing, but with shorter hair tied back with a bandana—sat on an old armchair. "Right through there," she said.

The toilet and tiny hand sink were in a space so small, Maureen's knees almost bumped the wall when she sat down, but any port in a storm. When she dried her hands, she noticed the paper towels were like the one she'd photographed—each folded in thirds, pulled out of a box like Kleenex, not torn off a roll.

Both women were sitting when she emerged, one still in the chair, the other on the small couch. Maureen had the odd sensation they'd been waiting for her to come find them.

"Thanks," she said. "Y'all saved me." She paused to look around. It seemed polite not to rush out. "You must be the cleaning ladies."

"I'm Deb and this is Linda," the first woman said.

"We're sisters, if you can't tell," Linda said. "And our mom, June, works here too. Two of us work every day, so the third one gets a day off. We switch it out."

"Good schedule," Maureen said, "as long as you don't have any family feuds."

They laughed. "No, we even all live together."

A studio portrait of a little girl in a red Christmas dress hung on the wall over the couch. "Cute baby," Maureen said.

"She's mine," Deb said. "But she thinks she has three moms. Linda's the one who spoils her."

"She's too sweet not to spoil," Linda said.

That was enough small talk. "You heard about the fire last night, I guess," Maureen said.

"Terry couldn't wait to tell us. He's the biggest gossip," Linda said. "And you're here to figure out what happened?"

"Yep. Can I ask you a couple of questions?"

They nodded in unison.

"Do all the rooms in the hotel have phone books?" Maureen asked.

It wasn't the question they expected, judging by the way their heads jerked.

"We put phone books in every room when new ones come out," Deb said.

"But half of them disappear before the year is up," Linda said. "Who knows why?"

"How about these?" Maureen held up the paper towel she'd dried her hands on. "Are these in all the rooms?"

"They're in all the kitchenettes," Deb said.

So not a vagrant with a cigarette, or a homeless person starting a campfire.

"Are any of your cleaning supplies flammable?"

"We use kerosene to remove spots sometimes," Linda said. "Why do you want to know?"

If Maureen told them why, she knew Terry would hear about it. And probably Joe, too, since Terry was a gossip. Was that good or bad? Better err on the side of caution. "Sorry, I can't say. It could be a police matter."

That would give them all plenty to speculate about.

16

Maureen left her film for developing. When she got home, she called J.J. Ralston, who was off duty but expected to hear from her and told him what she'd seen, what had fueled the fire, the easy availability of at least one accelerant. Then it was up to him to decide whether or not to get the police involved.

J.J. grunted. "Yeah, pretty much what I expected. Will I get your report on Monday?'

"With photos."

Maureen didn't know exactly how what she had to say met J.J.'s expectations, but she hung up knowing she'd done the job. She'd get paid. She was pretty sure it would end there, though, since the fire hadn't amounted to anything. J.J. was probably settling down to watch a ballgame on TV, not to ponder last night's puny little fire.

She checked her mail. She hoped for a couple of checks, but it was all catalogues, a flyer from a new car wash, and an electric bill. Oh well.

She should type up her report while the scene was fresh in her mind, but if it wasn't urgent to J.J., why hurry? How long since she'd gotten some exercise? A week? No, since Sunday. Six days. A run would feel good. Later.

First, she'd do something else she'd let slip too long. She called a couple of old friends to see if they wanted to meet for a drink later. Lucy was always on her about not staying in touch, but Lucy didn't answer, so Maureen left a message.

Sheila picked up on the first ring. "Maureen? Oh, I thought it was Holly." Holly was Sheila's daughter. "The baby's due any minute. I'm on my way out the door now."

Baby? Oh yeah, the last few times Maureen had seen her, Sheila was over the moon about becoming a grandmother, but for real? If Sheila was old enough, then so was Maureen—if she'd gotten started early the way Sheila had—and that was too crazy to think about. Marriage wouldn't have been impossible if Maureen had put her mind to it. But kids? Never.

"I'm staying in Richmond as long as they'll let me," Sheila was saying. "I'll call you when I get back."

No more excuses for putting off work. Maureen fed a report form into the typewriter waiting on the kitchen table and stared at it. What to say?

Somebody had grabbed paper towels and a phone book from the hotel, picked up twigs nearby, bothered to make a circle of rocks, added a dash of something to get the fire going, struck a match, and whoosh. If the fire hadn't gotten up into the pine branches, it would have burned itself out fast.

That much was all clear enough, as she had told J.J. All she needed to do was put it on paper. But there was something stopping her, like a shape in and out of peripheral vision, unfocused but distracting.

Maureen's stomach growled. OK, eat now, work later.

She pushed the typewriter away, went to the refrigerator, pulled out a tub of tuna salad and a loaf of bread. She made a sandwich and pondered, a beer or a Coke? The beer would be an admission that she wouldn't run later. She sighed and went with Coke.

After she had shut Joe down that morning by telling him she had to get to work, he'd looked so pitiful she had to feel sorry for him. She'd asked him one last question. "In as few words as possible, Joe, can you tell me exactly what you did see?"

He'd taken no notice of the few words part. "Do you believe in fate, Maureen? Was it purely random I got off the interstate where I did, or that this hotel was the first one I came to? Or that something told me not to go to sleep early?"

"Joe—" she said.

He held up a hand. "Hang on. I'm getting there. Last night, I did doze a little, sitting in my chair by the window, but something woke me up in time, and I saw those flames. I grabbed the phone, told Terry to call for help, then I ran down as fast as I could. Didn't want to wait on the elevator. My feet hardly touched those stairs, I swear, and headed for the back door. When I went past the elevator, I heard it humming, the way they do when they're on the move. It was going up. I watched. It went to the third floor. The third floor, Maureen. It had to be Cubby going back up after he set that fire." He'd looked triumphant, like he'd broken the crime of the century.

Maybe he had.

She found a jar of bread-and-butter pickles and added them to her sandwich. She did wonder why a man would leave a warm bed with a woman in it to go out and set a fire. And then there was that second phone call to 911. Who and why?

The answer rose to the surface like one of those Magic 8 Ball toys: Cubby did it to impress the woman. The pretty lady. And she made the call.

17

Cubby drove out of the gas station parking lot and turned toward Littleboro. Lammie did not want to go home. She curled her legs onto the car seat and laid her head on his right thigh.

"Now don't start anything," he said. "You don't want me to drive off the road."

She felt the rise and fall of his muscles, his bones, the shift of his joints all the way down to his toes. She felt the tires on the macadam vibrate through his sinews. She closed her eyes.

The sudden lack of motion woke her.

"Hey," Cubby whispered. "Hate to wake you, but we're here."

Lammie sat up, smoothed her skirt, looked around. The house she'd grown up in seemed smaller than it had the day before, drabber. There was an unfamiliar white pickup in the driveway, and a man she'd never seen before was using clippers on the straggly boxwoods around the foundation. Maybe it wasn't the same house at all. Maybe the world had changed in a single night, and she didn't live here anymore.

Then Mama stepped out onto the front porch and waved. Cubby got out of the car and came around to open Lammie's door. "Who's that man?" he asked.

"I have no idea." She took Cubby's hand and got out of the car.

Mama called something to the man. He turned around to look toward Lammie and Cubby and tilted the gray felt hat he wore onto the back of his head. A high forehead without a hairline in sight. Tall, lanky. Brown corduroy pants and a white sweatshirt with flecks of leaves stuck to it. Mama stepped off the porch and came to stand beside him.

"About time you got here," she called. "Come meet Len."

Lammie didn't move until Cubby put his hand on the small of her back and nudged her up the sidewalk toward the porch.

"Len Ogden," the man said. He extended his hand to Cubby.

"Quinn Tatum." Cubby shook hands. He turned to Mama. "It's nice to see you, Miss Mary Ruth. Hope you're well."

Mama's lips pressed into a thin line. "Yes, thank you."

Lammie knew that tone of voice. Mama thought disapproval was a little knife that nicked, but its edge had long-since blunted, as far as Lammie was concerned.

"And you're Lammie," Len said. "You're the image of Miss Mary Ruth." He smiled and nodded toward Mama. "Could be sisters."

Lammie wanted to roll her eyes but managed a close-lipped smile of her own.

"Len was my dinner date last night," Mama said. "When he picked me up and saw the state of this yard, he insisted he'd come back today and clean it up some."

"That's very nice, Mr. Ogden," Lammie said.

Mama had had a date? She'd not said anything about that. But then Lammie hadn't said anything about Cubby either. Just left a note, "I won't be home tonight," when she'd gone home at lunch to get her overnight bad, knowing Mama would be out.

"Isn't it?" Mama said. She tilted her head toward the man and smiled. "Have y'all eaten? I'm fixing Len a snack."

"Thank you, Miss Mary Ruth," Cubby said. "We've eaten, and Aunt Dru will be looking for me."

"Yes, I'm sure she will," Mama said. The little knife again.

"Let me carry this to the house for you, Lammie." Cubby held the overnight bag. He put his hand on the small of Lammie's back again. "Good to meet you, Len."

Lammie walked ahead of him into the house. They were alone in the dim front hall. She took the bag from him, dropped it, and stepped into his embrace. "When do I see you again?"

"I have more business to do this week—Dad's estate and all. Next Friday?"

"Not till Friday?" Last week had seemed so long, did she have to endure another one?

"I'll be thinking about you every minute." He held her for a long moment.

Two people who keep secrets, he'd said. And that made them indispensable to each other. Didn't it?

He stepped away, and she felt a flick of panic. His gaze stayed steady on her face, and the panic ebbed.

"Mama will be coming in," she said and gave him a gentle push. "Go on. I'll be all right. Till Friday."

One quick kiss and he turned toward the door. When it closed behind him, she grabbed her bag and ran upstairs. From her bedroom window, she saw him talking to Mama again. He waved to Len Ogden, got in the Caddy, and drove away. His absence hurt.

She closed her eyes and remembered how the brilliant flames had thrilled her. That memory made her think again of the lights and chaos the night Daddy was shot, there in the front yard where Len Ogden stood with Mama now. She opened her eyes and saw Len must have finished the boxwoods because he carried his clippers to the truck and got out a rake. Mama disappeared under the porch roof, coming inside.

"Lammie," Mama called from downstairs, "I could use some help." She'd want to talk, to pry, to scold.

Lammie didn't answer. She looked around the bedroom. How had Cubby seen it, that first time they were together? Was it too much pink? Were there too many ruffles? Was it stifling? No, he hadn't even noticed—they'd been too caught up in each other, she was sure about that.

She wanted to let herself into the secret room. She could open a shoe box, add the money she'd collected during the past week, and riffle the edges of the bills, the thing she had done for so long whenever she needed to feel safe. She thought about what Cubby had said, how once fire had calmed him, how it had been his medicine. Now she understood just what he meant.

But she was afraid to go in just now, afraid Mama would come up looking for her, and sure enough, there was Mama tapping on the door.

"Lammie, did you hear me?"

Lammie opened the door a crack but did not step aside for Mama to come in. "What?"

"You could help me make sandwiches," Mama said.

"It doesn't take two people to make sandwiches."

"I want you to get to know Len and have a nice conversation. Try to make up for the fact that you just embarrassed yourself and me by announcing to the world you spent the night with a man."

"I'm not embarrassed."

Mama peered past Lammie, as if there was something to see. When Lammie didn't budge, she sighed. "All right. I know you're a grown woman. I know you're hardly an innocent, but I did think more of Cubby. His mother would be shocked."

Lammie half expected her to follow up with, "What would your daddy think?" But she didn't.

"All right. You come on down when you're ready."

Lammie unpacked her things, the blouse and suit jacket she'd worn to work the day before, the black lace bra and panties. The black silk slip. She rubbed the slip against her cheek and inhaled the scents of Cubby and their lovemaking. She would take an afternoon off and go shopping. She needed to replenish her supply of lingerie before Friday and think of more ways to surprise Cubby.

Maybe while she was shopping, she'd look for a new bedspread. Or stop at the hardware and get paint samples. But what if she didn't stay here forever? It had been years since she'd had that thought.

She couldn't hide much longer, or Mama would be back, so she set her face into the look she wore in the office every day and went downstairs.

Mama had made a pot of hot tea in a china pot. Whenever had she made hot tea? Or used the china? A plate of pimento cheese sandwiches cut in quarters sat on the coffee table in the front room. Mama sat on the sofa, and Len sat in the same armchair where Lammie had waited for Cubby. Was that just a week earlier?

"Lammie," Mama said to her, "come sit with us. I have a cup for you." She poured. "Len, tell Lammie something about yourself."

"Not much to tell," he said, and then went on to tell. He was a widower, just moved to town to live near his daughter and her family. Retired engineer. Thought he'd like Littleboro just fine. When he said that, he and Mama locked eyes for a moment, until Mama turned girlish and looked down.

Well, well. What made Lammie smile was knowing that a few weeks ago, she'd have felt ill, turned her back, walked away from the idea of Mama and a man. Now, it made no difference. Good for Mama. And Len was welcome to her.

"When did you two meet?" Lammie asked. Not because she was interested.

"A month ago," Mama said. "His son-in-law is…"

Lammie tuned it out. Something about one of Mama's bookkeeping clients and how if she'd been five minutes later that day, they wouldn't have crossed paths. Mama didn't say fate or destiny, but that's what she was thinking. Good luck to Len. At least he was enjoying the pimento cheese.

When he was gone, Mama said, "Now that's a gentleman."

"What's your point, Mama?"

"That note you left. Five words. How was I supposed to know where you were, or who with? I'm your mother, but you never tell me anything." She picked up the empty sandwich plate and teapot. "Bring those cups and saucers."

Lammie picked them up and followed her mother to the kitchen. "Why should I tell you anything, Mama? Just because we live under the same roof?"

The last time Lammie told her something important, everything that mattered to her just then, Mama had turned her back, walked out of the room, not spoken to her again for days. Why would she expect Lammie to confide after that?

"I let you come home when everybody knew you'd disgraced yourself. I didn't have to do that. You never even thanked me." Mama set the teapot down so hard, its lid rattled.

Better not show Len that temper too soon. And the bourbon bottle hadn't even come out yet. Lammie smiled.

"What's so funny?"

"Nothing, Mama." Lammie turned around to leave the room.

"Lammie," Mama said. "Please—"

Something in her tone of voice made Lammie stop at the door.

"I didn't mean to pick a fight," Mama said. "I worry about you. The man's been gone for more than twenty years. What do you know about him now? He's not the boy you mooned after in high school."

Mooned after? If Mama had known that, she'd never let on.

Lammie faced her. "Not long ago you were telling me I ought to go after him, he'd be a catch."

Mama flipped a dish towel, flipping away her own words. "I didn't know you were going to throw yourself at him. And have you asked him why he never married? I suppose he says he never met the right girl. That's what they always say."

"They who? What are you implying?"

"You need to be careful, that's all."

The telephone rang. Mama glared at it like she was not ready to quit the battlefield she'd created, but the phone won, and she answered.

"Oh, Helen, yes, Len showed me the nicest time." Mama turned her back to Lammie.

Lammie had to get out of the kitchen, but—it was strange—she didn't want to be in her room either. The front porch swing was as far as she got. The sun was off the yard now, the day losing warmth. Mama would be telling Helen everything, how Lammie treated her badly, how Lammie had behaved with Cubby and wasn't even ashamed, and Helen would be going, Yes, yes, Mary Ruth, you are a saint.

No, she hadn't asked Cubby that question about marriage, other women. Hadn't felt the need to. He hadn't asked her either. That was the past. Just like her own history—over and done with. Ashes.

Lammie closed her eyes. If Cubby were to drive up right this minute, she'd run to him, get in the car, and he'd take her away, far away. But no, she couldn't leave the money behind. And nothing Mama said or did mattered anymore anyway.

When she opened her eyes, she saw Miss Leora in her front yard, puttering in her rose bed. Year-round, even when those rose bushes looked like naked, thorny sticks in the ground, Miss Leora found something to do to them. She saw Lammie now and raised her hand to wave. Lammie waved back and felt—what? That it wasn't Miss Leora's fault she believed Lammie slept through everything the night Daddy died and told Mama that, so forever after Mama could pretend it was true? Miss Leora meant to be kind. Why had Lammie never thought of that before?

She stopped the motion of the swing, got up, went inside. Mama was still on the phone, laughing now, so not talking about her. She had nowhere to go but upstairs.

18

For Maureen, Saturday night was an old movie on TV, spaghetti with sauce from a jar, most of a bottle of red wine.

Sunday meant sleeping late. Laundry. Groceries. That run, finally. And time to think about work, whether she wanted to or not. Was there enough coming up? Too much? The first of the month was coming. There would be bills to pay.

If she wanted to get paid for the jobs of the last couple of days, she needed to take care of business. First, she got the invoice for the trip to Farmer Big Tom's together. Mileage, meals while in transit—including her birthday dinner at the coast—hours traveled—tedious but easy.

Then back to the Highway Home fire.

She fed the report form she'd started the day before back into the typewriter, and her fingers froze again. Joe Corcoran's voice was in her head. What if the firebug does it again? he'd asked. She had to agree. If it was a firebug, it was likely he would do it again.

What else Joe had said, that's what had kept her from finishing the report. That stuff about not seeing but still knowing, having a feeling, fate putting him there, and how she and he were alike. Not that they were. No way.

What if she put suspicions and hunches—Joe's feelings, her tingles—down on paper? If she did, J.J. would never take her seriously again. If she hand-delivered the report, she could tell him she was worried the fire might not be the last, or the first, for that matter. He could check to see if there were dots to connect. Not putting her thoughts in writing would keep them from being on the official record. Even if he rolled his eyes, he'd have to hear what she said.

She left the report again, changed into sweats, and laced up her running shoes. Because anything was better than stewing over a stupid little fire that didn't do any damage. Or some wacky guy who lived in a van, who might even be gone by now.

After the run, she decided to scramble eggs and make toast for supper. She turned on the portable TV in the kitchen to catch a weather forecast and instead got a special live report: a major fire at the construction site for a new industrial park on the north side of the city.

She froze, an egg in each hand, to watch the live feed from the scene. The reporter was excited, talking over himself with a chaotic scene in the background. Multiple fire stations responding. Construction vehicles and large equipment in flames. Piles of lumber and material burning. The contractor's trailer involved. Since it was Sunday, no work was going on, but two men who provided security were unaccounted for.

Maureen was aware of the project. Anyone who drove by it over the three years it had been under construction had to be. Roads closed, detours that shifted all the time, acres of what had been farmland chewed up, fencing that looked like it belonged around a prison, not a building site.

The reporter recapped the history. The project had been approved by the city council by one vote after months of debate. The developers had been sued several times, paid fines, and kept going. Demonstrators had chained themselves to trees while there were trees still standing, then to the gates in the fencing. Could the fire be ecoterrorism? Neighbors half a mile away reported hearing explosions.

Ecoterrorism? That was a new thing for Raleigh. Maureen broke the eggs into a bowl and stirred them with a fork. The investigation into this fire would be huge. SBI for sure. Probably ATF. She could imagine herself walking into the hellscape that would be left, one of the dozens of people it would take to investigate. Where would they start? How many points of ignition would they find? But there was no chance she'd be part of it.

She melted butter in a skillet. One thing for sure—J.J. Ralston and the rest of RFD would be so busy for the weeks to come, the Highway Home's puny blaze would not get another thought. It didn't matter what she put in her report. She would finish it and go to bed early. It looked like a slow week ahead, though an empty calendar didn't mean much. Just look at the last few days.

By Monday morning, she had shoved Joe and thoughts about Joe into a closet and slammed the door. She picked up her photos and added some to the envelope with her report and invoice. Had she told J.J. she would deliver it in person? She wasn't sure, but she was sure that he'd barely glance at it now anyway. She went to the post office, stood in a short line to have the envelope weighed, and when the clerk dropped it into a bin behind him, she figured she'd heard the last of the Highway Home, Joe Corcoran, and the firebug—if there was one.

She headed for home and ran into a slow-down due to road construction. Not what she needed, time to drum her fingers on the steering wheel and think, whether she wanted to or not. If it was a firebug, what made her think this was the first time they'd done it?

Now that was an interesting question. Had there been any other low-level fires around Raleigh recently, too low-level for anybody to bother putting them together? Or maybe out in the county? Nearby counties? Terry told her this Mr. Tatum was from Littleboro. Nearby as it was, she'd never been there.

It was still early in the day, and now she had a plan.

Maureen bothered to put a few hot rollers in her hair so they could do whatever they did while she changed into a pair of navy pants and a white blouse. She dabbed on enough makeup to make it look like she cared. It was what people expected of a woman. When she took out the rollers, she was disappointed but not surprised at the lack of even a wave. She pulled her hair into a low ponytail—softer than her usual look—and put on a light blue jacket. Gold hoop earrings. Lipstick. Not bad, she thought.

She studied her well-worn road map to figure out exactly how to get to Littleboro. It wasn't direct. East on the interstate, then angle back south and west. Experience told her the fire department wouldn't be hard to find.

Raleigh morning traffic had thinned, so it only took her twenty minutes to get to the exit off the interstate. Littleboro would be one more small town that got smaller when new highways passed it by. She'd seen a lot of them. Odd, the town wasn't mentioned on the exit signs. She didn't doubt her own map-reading skills, though, so she took the ramp and turned right.

The state, then county roads went past small farms, country stores, and white churches with stubby steeples. When she passed a Piggly Wiggly and a Rose's Store, she knew she was close to civilization. One more curve and she saw the town limits sign. Welcome to Littleboro, The Little Town Time Forgot.

There was a small development of ranch and split-level houses, Something Estates, just inside the town limits. She drove past older houses, then a string of small businesses, then saw the backside of a broad three-story brick building. The courthouse, no doubt. The street took a zig and a zag, and she was on the courthouse square. Big old oaks, a statue in the middle, with two- and three-story office buildings and shops on the streets that made the square. All familiar from other small-town county seats.

She made a right, then a left, and saw a sign pointing to the fire department, a block to the west. All three visitors' parking places were open, so she took the one closest to the door, got her briefcase out of the back seat, straightened her jacket, and walked in.

"Yes, ma'am?" A man in uniform sat behind the desk. "Can we help you?"

"I'd like to speak to the chief." She took a card from her

pocket and handed it to the man.

He studied it, then leaned back in his chair, craned his neck, and called, "Chief, somebody to see you."

"Send 'em in." The voice came from an open office door.

"Step right on in, ma'am," the man said.

Maureen went in the direction of the disembodied voice. The chief stood up to greet her. She extended her hand to shake his and got his name, Shepard, from the badge on his shirt pocket. Tallish, in his forties, fit-looking. razor-sharp jawline, light brown eyes, darker brown hair. The best-looking man she'd seen in a while. Quite a while. If Maureen had a type, he was it.

She brought that line of thought to a screeching halt. Business, business, business.

"Chief Shepard, I'm Maureen Boykin. I'm an independent fire investigator. I'd like you to have my credentials in case you ever need to call somebody in."

"Glad to meet you, ma'am." He gestured to the visitor's chair and waited until she sat to seat himself again.

"Thank you," she said. "I won't take too much of your time." She had a second card stapled to a resumé with her degrees in chemistry and physics, specialized training, experience, and references from insurance companies and fire departments she'd worked for. Shepard took it from her and looked it over.

"It's an unusual occupation for a lady, isn't it?" he said. "But it looks like you know your stuff."

She ignored the "unusual" and the "lady" and launched into her standard presentation, pretty much what the resumé said. If she read Shepard right, he'd appreciate a brisk but not hard tone.

He listened, made eye contact, began nodding halfway

through. "I can't say we'll have a reason to call on you, Miss Boykin, but you never know. I'll keep this handy."

Now she could ask her questions. "Have you had any odd fires lately, maybe not much property damage done, but not quite explained either?"

"Can't think of any like that. Not lately."

"I've been called to several," she said, and leaned forward. One, several. All the same. "I'm beginning to think there could be a pattern."

"Is that right?" He matched her lean.

"I can't make it official yet, but I understand what you chiefs are up against, budgets and all that. It can be tricky to put two and two together, so I'm monitoring any suspicious fires in the counties around Wake."

"Monitoring? You're working for somebody on that?"

"I can't disclose at the moment." She shrugged an I-would-if-I-could shrug. "I hope you'll call me if you come across anything." She stood and so did Shepard.

"I will, for sure. I'll put some feelers out, in case somebody has had an odd fire and didn't bother calling us."

"That's perfect. Just what I'm needing."

"You're from Raleigh?" He studied her card again. "That fire over the weekend was sure something."

"At the industrial park? I've never been involved in anything that big. Have you?"

"No." He'd had a professional deadpan until then. It slipped when he grinned. "We can hope, right?"

They shook hands again. She'd kept her eyes on his face while they talked. Now she took a quick look around. Behind him on a cabinet was a framed photograph of two children, a girl and boy, sitting side by side on a bench. So he was a dad. That meant there was a mom somewhere.

Not surprising. And just her luck.

She got back into her car and paused to think. It had gone well, though she had no way of knowing if he was holding anything back. Her senses said no, but she checked herself. That was what she wanted to believe.

Her stomach told her, it was lunchtime. She drove back to the square and spotted the Legal Eagle Café. She found a parking place on a side street and began walking toward the restaurant. She stopped dead. A tan and green camper van rumbled past her. Joe Corcoran's camper van? What the heck?

She saw Joe plain as day, but he didn't see her. He went around the same corner she had taken, no doubt looking for a parking space of his own. She would wait two or three minutes, right where she was. And sure enough, about the time she expected him, he showed up, walking toward her. When he saw her, he stopped short just as she had, then shook his head, grinned a little, and closed the gap.

"What are you doing here?" he asked.

"I'm going to the café. It's lunch time."

"I guess it is," he said. "But that's not exactly what I meant."

She turned and they went in, side by side. She didn't say anything else until they were at a back booth with laminated menus in front of them.

"Well?" he asked.

She smiled to herself. She'd gotten him to speak first. "I had business with the local fire chief." She skimmed the menu. "How about you?"

"Nice day for a drive in the country." He studied the menu, didn't look up.

Mr. Cool, huh? That was a change from the guy eager to

share his theories a couple of days earlier.

The waitress was young, late teens. She wore a lot of blue eye shadow and pink lipstick that set Maureen's teeth on edge, but she had a good smile for newcomers. "What can I get y'all?"

"The chicken salad plate and a yeast roll, please. Iced tea," Maureen said.

"Two hot dogs, one with chili and slaw, one with mustard and relish. Fries," Joe said. "A Coke."

The girl nodded as if they'd both picked her favorites.

"Do you know a man named Cubby?" Joe asked as she took the menu from him.

Maureen wanted to kick him for asking flat out like that. But if he was going to ask, he should get it right. "Quinn Tatum," she said.

The girl nodded. "I know who you mean. My mama went to his daddy's funeral a couple of weeks ago. She came home and told my daddy that Quinn Tatum is handsome as ever." She rolled her eyes. "I think they dated or something a long time ago. I better get these orders in for you."

"Well now." Joe looked smug.

"Well now what?" Maureen pulled napkins out of the dispenser and arranged them on her lap.

"Filling in the blanks."

"When she comes back, you can ask her to ask her mama if Quinn Tatum was named most likely to become an arsonist in their yearbook."

"You know what?" Joe said. "He hasn't been back to the Highway Home since he left Saturday. That's what they call consciousness of guilt."

Where the heck had Joe picked that up? Cop shows, probably. "Meaning?"

"Well, if I'd gotten away with something like he did, I'd stay as far from the scene of the crime as I could, right?"

"I thought criminals return to the scene."

The waitress brought their drinks and silverware.

"Thanks. Callie, is it?" Joe peered at her nametag. "You happen to know where the Tatums live?"

"Are you friends of theirs?"

Maybe she was shrewd enough not to answer him, Maureen thought. Wouldn't friends already know where Quinn Tatum lived?

"Used to be," Joe said. "We lost touch."

"They have the big white house just outside town. Near the lake." Callie turned her head in response to a bell ringing. "Your order's ready. Be right back."

Maureen whispered across the table. "What if she goes home and tells her mother strangers were asking about Quinn Tatum, and word gets back to him?"

"So?"

"Maybe she describes you to her mom and Tatum hears about it. Maybe he recognizes the description because of the run-in you said you two had." It sounded far-fetched, but then so did a lot of what Joe had said.

"So?" Joe grinned at her.

"So, you've just tipped off the guy we suspect of being an arsonist. He could leave town. Or he knows where you're staying. He could come after you."

"You always worry this much about things that haven't happened?"

Callie delivered their plates and moved to a table of newcomers who seemed to be regulars.

Joe squirted ketchup on his fries, studied his hot dogs, and opted for the mustard and relish one first. "Did I just hear you say we suspect him? You're coming around to my way of thinking, huh?"

Maureen peppered her chicken salad, squeezed lemon into her tea. No way was she going to answer that question.

"What was your business with the fire chief, anyway?" Joe said.

All right. How could it hurt to tell him? "I asked if there had been any unusual fires around here. And the answer is, no."

"Huh." He finished his first hot dog and moved onto the second.

19

By Monday morning, Lammie had a plan for the week. She told Attorney Morton she would need Wednesday afternoon off for some personal business. That evening, she told Mama she needed the car Wednesday to drive to Raleigh on business for Attorney Morton.

Tuesday night, she took one hundred dollars out of the latest shoebox. She'd never taken money out before, and it made her heart beat like a bird's—but it was time to put it to use. She rolled the bills tight, wrapped a rubber band around the roll, and nestled it among the lipstick, comb, and compact she carried in a zippered bag in her purse. She eased herself into dreamy sleep.

Wednesday morning, at quarter of nine, the office door opened, and Joy of Joy's Florals came in.

"Oh good, you're here. I have another delivery for you, Lammie." She set a milk glass vase on the desk and fluffed the three red roses, baby's breath, and fern fronds it contained. "Third one for you this week. I thought I'd better bring it myself."

"Thank you." Lammie tried not to blush, not to smile, not to fuel Joy's smug attitude.

"He is a smitten man if I've ever seen one." Joy craned her neck to look at the two matching vases that sat on the credenza behind Lammie, one with five roses, one with four. "I see the others are holding up well. When he placed the orders Monday, I asked him, what's the countdown for? He was very mysterious, wouldn't say."

Lammie didn't intend to say either, but she knew. She rubbed one of the velvety petals between her forefinger and thumb. Let Joy simmer.

"You ought to dry the roses. Nice keepsakes. I have little kits for doing that in the store. Want me to bring you one with tomorrow's order?"

Was Lammie the type of woman who showed her grandchildren the first roses their papaw ever gave her? By then, the flowers would be faded to brown, petals leathery. No, she was not that woman.

"No thank you, Joy. I can manage."

Joy sighed. "Well, I can tell you, you're the only girl in town getting flowers every day this week."

When Joy was gone, Lammie moved the vase into line with the others. Deep red, rose red. Maybe the lingerie shop would have something that color. A corset, maybe. Garters. White stockings.

It was nice Cubby had a romantic side to him, but if he asked her, she'd say the flowers weren't important. Joy would spread the word all over town that Lammie Timmons and Quinn Tatum were an item. That wasn't important either.

What mattered was Cubby. And fire. And the two of them together.

Attorney Morton had a regular Wednesday morning breakfast meeting with the committee planning Littleboro's celebration of America's bicentennial. Every time he came back, he had work for Lammie to do. Order the bunting. Write something for the newspaper. Call potential sponsors. She'd be glad when the Fourth of July had come and gone.

"Good morning, Lammie." When Attorney Morton bustled into the office at ten o'clock, he was smiling and flushed as if he'd drunk something besides coffee that morning. How could talk about floats and the high school marching band make him that giddy?

"Did any reporters call yet?" He rested his briefcase on her desk.

"Reporters? About the bicentennial? No. Should they?"

"No, no. Something else even more exciting. Word gets out, you know." He shifted his feet like a little boy, waiting to be coaxed.

Lord help her. "What word would that be?"

"Senator Wayland is going to run for lieutenant governor. I'm going to be his campaign chairman."

Lammie drew a deep breath. In the years she'd worked for him—ever since the senator had exiled her from Raleigh to Littleboro— Attorney Morton had never spoken Wayland's name to her. It had to be because he knew their history and was sworn to secrecy. The men were friends, she knew, and involved in politics together, but she was never asked to place his calls to Wayland. And the senator never placed calls to anyone himself, so Lammie did not have to hear his voice, just his secretary saying, "Senator Wayland for Mr. Morton."

"Now, Lammie," Attorney Morton said, "don't look that way. Surely after all this time—it's water under the bridge, over the dam, isn't it?"

"You took me by surprise, that's all." Morton may not be overly bright, but he wasn't mean. She put on her office face. "I left a few messages on your desk. I'll get your coffee."

"You know I count on you, Lammie." He picked up his briefcase and headed for his office. "And I'm going to need you helping me to keep everything organized."

She paused in the break room to rest her head against the wall and take a few deep breaths. She filled a coffee cup, added cream and sugar, and carried it to her boss.

The next phone call was indeed from a reporter, wanting a statement from the rumored candidate's campaign manager. She put him right through.

A few minutes later, Attorney Morton emerged from his office and set a cardboard box on Lammie's desk.

"State party letterhead stationery," he said. "And here"—he handed her several pages from a legal pad—"is a press release. You can fix it up for me, like you always do. It needs to go out to all the newspapers in the state this afternoon."

His loopy old-fashioned script filled three sheets off a legal pad. She pursed her lips. "Have you forgotten I plan to take this afternoon off for personal business?"

"But this is important, Lammie. How about tomorrow for your business? I'll give you the whole day off."

"I'm sorry, Mr. Morton, but my business is urgent."

She didn't want to get involved in his politics.

She sure didn't want the senator back in her life.

Her boss grumbled, tried again. "Now see here, Lammie," but had nothing to complete the sentence with.

A little later, as he left for a lunch meeting, she let him see a sheet of party letterhead was in her typewriter. She smiled and patted his handwritten statement to show everything was under control. "I'll have this done before I go."

The statement was silly. A press release to announce that an announcement would be made in ten days. And that announcement was to be, Senator Wayland would run for his first statewide office. The campaign would be chaired by A. Carlyle Morton, Esquire. She noticed Morton's name appeared more times than the candidate's.

Lammie rewrote it the way she always rewrote Morton's letters and the little speeches he gave to civic groups. She laid the page on his desk, so he'd see it first thing. He'd be proud of how articulate he was. Everybody would say he did a fine job.

Her car was parked behind the building. When she drove past the square, she got a glimpse of Attorney Morton talking to two other men. He was too busy being important to see her.

State Senator Harold Wayland was already a powerful man on his way to becoming the majority leader when Lammie went to work for him. He'd be governor eventually, people had said, when his turn came. When Lammie had finished her courses to become a legal secretary, the college's placement office sent her to the legislative building to apply for a job. Lammie had commuted the forty-five minutes from

Littleboro for her classes, but she had agreed to share an apartment in Raleigh with another girl, once they both found jobs.

Mama hadn't been happy about that, but Lammie was happier than she'd been in her whole life when she and Shelley were both hired by state government, when they split the cost of curtains, pots and pans, and a plaid area rug. The rest of the furniture came from Shelley's parents' attic. Shelley spent more nights with her boyfriend than she did at the apartment, and that suited Lammie too.

After she'd been working in the senator's office for six weeks, there was another reason to be glad Shelley wasn't around. Lammie didn't want to explain her comings and goings to a roommate, or the late-night phone calls or the guest who came to visit at all hours, always on short notice.

At work, Lammie got promoted quickly, and people whispered. She ignored them. Years later, it occurred to her the older woman who was the senator's secretary wasn't jealous after all. She was trying to warn Lammie. Maybe even protect her. It was too late for that.

Then it was over. She never knew why it ended when it did. Suddenly Senator Wayland didn't call her after hours with a low "hey, sweetheart," or slip a "miss you" or "thinking about you" note into the pile of papers he handed her, or ask her to find an excuse to interrupt a committee meeting "just so I can see you."

Had all that stopped after his wife came in one afternoon, marched straight to his office, closed the door, and marched out again ten minutes later, not saying a word to anybody?

Or was it when the new prettier girl started work?

When the senator did ask to see her after a few weeks—it seemed like forever—it was to say his old friend Carlyle Morton—she must know him from her hometown—needed a crackerjack legal assistant and it would be a great job for her.

Lammie packed her bags and abandoned her half of the plaid rug. She didn't tell Mama she was coming, just hired her landlord's son to drive her and her belongings back to Littleboro.

Mama welcomed her with hugs and smiles, then looked her in the face and asked, "What's wrong?"

They were in the kitchen, and when Lammie began to cry, Mama eased her into a chair at the table, smoothed her hair, wrapped her arms around her until she could talk again. Then she told Mama everything. The senator. That she'd thought he loved her. He'd said so. She thought they had a future. And then, and then—more tears, endless-seeming tears.

It took moments to realize Mama had let go, had pulled away, was staring at her but also past her at some faraway thing. When Lammie looked up at her, Mama was like a statue. Cold, hard.

"How could you?" Mama said. "A married man." Then she pivoted, turned her back to Lammie, and left the room. They didn't speak for three days.

Mama had always said the news stories about Daddy getting shot because he was having an affair weren't true. She said everybody knew that awful man beat his wife, and George Timmons only tried to help her because he was kind and decent.

Lammie's tears dried up and left her with a pounding headache. She went to her room, closed the curtains, and lay down without undressing. She knew from the way Mama iced her out, Mama had lied to her and everybody. Daddy had done what the man said.

Lammie swore to herself she'd never cry again.

Not long after, she read Cubby's inscription in the yearbook. Not long after that, she had her first five dollars to add to Granny's money.

Lammie followed the roads Cubby had driven to reach the interstate. She thought about the Friday night past and thought about the Friday night to come. Just two days away now.

She always bought her special lingerie at a small, elegant shop tucked away near downtown Raleigh. She had first gone there years ago when she worked for the senator, when he was treating her so sweetly. The store's owner called her at the office and told her an admirer had set up a credit account for her. At the time, it had given Lammie a sense that her life was a racy, romantic movie. The movie ended like a car going off a cliff, at least for her.

She'd thought about getting rid of the bra-and-panty sets and camisoles when it ended, but when she touched them, she decided she deserved them. She put them away in the little Samsonite suitcase in her secret room.

Over the years, she sometimes returned to the shop and bought things, even though nobody was likely to see them. She put them on in secret sometimes, even wore a little silky thing under a business suit sometimes. The shop treated its clientele with complete discretion, and as the owner—who, Lammie guessed, had opened another account for another girl for the same admirer soon enough—liked to murmur, we do it for ourselves anyway, don't we?

Lammie knew what she meant. Something secret under her go-to-court suit made her stand up taller and claim a little more power from the men who bustled and blustered around her.

And now she had Cubby to appreciate special things.

But as she drove past the legislative building and the old capitol and made the turn onto the shady side street, she felt slightly carsick. Was she going backwards in her life, instead of forward?

20

Lammie left the lingerie shop with a tiny buzz from the champagne the owner had offered her and a bigger buzz from the sensations of silk and lace against her skin. A leopard-print bra-and-panties set. A fuchsia camisole trimmed in lime green. And yes, a rose-red corset laced with black ribbons. All wrapped in tissue and laid like precious items in a black paper bag embossed with the Milady Shoppe logo and satin ribbon handles.

Which of the new purchases would she model for Cubby first? Maybe she'd treat him to a fashion show. The buzz grew.

Her car was in the small parking lot behind the shop, screened from the street by a privet hedge. Lammie slid behind the steering wheel and put her bag on the passenger's seat. She needed to settle herself before she started home. Maybe a drive through the tree-lined streets of old Raleigh. She closed her eyes and dreamed a moment, then put the key in the ignition and set out, no place special in mind.

A few minutes later, Lammie stopped her car in front of a wrought-iron gate in a red brick wall. The senator lived in a big white house behind that wall, a house invisible from the street.

She had been inside the gate twice, both times after the senator had left the office early, then realized he needed papers. Lammie had been dispatched to deliver them, was told to pull into the drive, then press a button on the brick pillar to alert someone in the house to open the gate for her. The gate had creaked, groaned, complained, reluctant to let her in, and then slammed behind her.

The paved driveway had wound through a perfectly mowed lawn. As she neared the house, a gravel track split off to the right. For deliveries, she imagined. Was she meant to go to the back door? Would she get fired if she did it wrong? She kept going to the front of the house. She pulled up to the wide stone steps and saw a Black man in a white jacket waiting on the broad porch. He came down the steps and took the papers from her through the driver's window. She did not even get out of the car.

The second time she made a delivery, no one waited on the porch. She stopped the car and, again, wondered what to do. Should she just sit until someone came? Blow the horn?

Instead, she turned off the engine, smoothed her hair, and went to the front door. She was surprised when the senator himself opened it. She'd worked in his office for a short time, and this was the first time she'd seen him outside of the legislative building. Instead of a severe suit and striped tie, he wore light gray pants, a rumpled cotton shirt open at the throat, and held a glass of brown liquid with ice cubes. His hair was tousled instead of slicked back. He looked younger. Almost young.

She held out the envelope. "Senator, you wanted this?"

He was looking at her as he never had, eyes up and down her. He smiled. "Yes, I believe I do."

Before long, it began. The thing between them.

It was spring, she remembered. The wide lawn had been edged by banks of azaleas the colors of watermelon and snow. Dogwoods and redbuds bloomed. All shades of white, cream, pink, red. Red like the new corset.

What if she pressed the button now? But that gate wouldn't open for her again. She sighed, and the tissue in the bag beside her seemed to sigh too. She heard the single polite beep of a horn. She looked in the rearview mirror and saw a large black car behind her, its turn signal on. She was blocking its way. It belonged there, she didn't.

She put her car in gear and moved past the entrance. The black car turned into the senator's drive. She imagined the driver's window lowering, a hand coming out to press the button, and the gate opening easily, smooth and welcoming to whoever was in that car.

Once she was out of the senator's neighborhood and on her way across the city, she was angry all over again. What would Cubby say if she told him how that man had used her, discarded her, and how she was now supposed to help him run for office? She missed light after light, stopping and starting, until she lost track of where she was.

She heard brakes squeal behind her. Horns blared. Lammie's heart slammed her ribs. She looked in her rearview mirror and saw two cars crossways in an intersection under the red light she'd just run, their front ends inches apart. She'd tuned the world out and almost caused an accident.

She pulled into a bank parking lot, shaking. She stopped and leaned her head against the steering wheel until she breathed normally again.

She drove slowly and carefully the rest of the way to Littleboro, forcing her mind to focus on her surroundings, on what was real. Still, any brake light in front of her, any truck pulling into her lane on the interstate made her stomach clinch. The ride back home with Cubby had passed in seconds. This one took forever. When she finally saw the courthouse ahead of her, the square beyond it, her shoulders slumped.

On Maple Street, Len Ogden's truck was in the driveway. No way Lammie wanted to sit and chat with her mother's new boyfriend. What would Cubby say if she turned up on his doorstep? Aunt Dru would be there wanting to talk about her late brother, buried just two weeks ago, about her sweet nephew's kindness letting her stay on in the house. And Cubby might not even be there. He'd said he had more work to do that week. Why hadn't she thought of it? He could be at the Highway Home right now. She could have gone there—but it was too late in the day to go back.

Her foot eased off the brake pedal, and she kept driving.

21

The first of the week, Joe was at loose ends, like the purpose of his life had wandered off, left him stranded. But he wasn't ready to chase it just yet. Despite his theory that Cubby wouldn't come back to the scene of his crime, the man showed up in the Caddy on Monday afternoon, alone. Cubby came and went from the Highway Home several times Tuesday. He wore a suit and carried a briefcase. Keeping up with him was practically a full-time job. Finally, Joe decided he needed to get out of the room, get some air.

He walked past the shopping center with the Chinese place and turned a corner down a street he hadn't been on before. He spotted a barbershop and ducked in for a trim.

Two of the four chairs were occupied. A third barber sat in his own chair, telling some story to the room. He broke off when he saw Joe.

"Come on in, mister. Have I seen you in here before?"

"No, sir, I'm passing through town. Saw your shop and thought I'd get myself tidied up."

"You came to the right place." The barber got up and gestured for Joe to take a seat. He was an older man, white-haired, tall, a little stooped, tending toward skinny.

"You remember how, Harvey?" one of the younger barbers said and got a laugh from the customers.

"Don't worry, mister." Harvey draped a cape over Joe's chest and shoulders. "I forgot more than this pup will ever know about cutting hair."

"Then it's my lucky day," Joe said.

Harvey spun the chair. "You look like a man who likes to keep it clean and short."

"You have me pegged." Joe studied the place reflected in the mirror. Plain, no frills, a bench like a church pew for men waiting a turn or loitering, the smell of soap and piney aftershave. He liked it, and he liked the way the men kidded each other. "I'm Joe, by the way."

While he worked, Harvey gave Joe his life's story. He was the former owner of the shop, and sold it to the two younger barbers, Pete and Jimmy, his nephews as a matter of fact, when his wife insisted he needed to retire.

"But I'm not too good at retirement, so I drop in here a few days a week to keep from going crazy. And be sure the boys are on the right track."

"Like I said," Joe said. "My lucky day."

"Where are you from, Joe?" the customer in the closest chair asked.

Joe explained about the camper van, about his travels, about going with his gut. "It got me here today."

"You're king of the road," one of the young barbers—Pete?—said, then sang a few lines from the old Roger

Miller song.

"That life sounds good to me," the other customer said. "No wife, no kids, no yard to mow, no bills to pay. Man, that sounds good." He was done with his haircut but in no hurry to leave.

"That's all true, but there's more to it," Joe said, "I meet people, usually when they're in trouble. I've changed more than one tire for somebody broke down by the side of the road. Or filled a gas tank when somebody ran out. It makes me feel good."

He got a round of attaboys for his good deeds. There was a lull while Harvey tilted Joe's head forward so he could trim the back. Snip of scissors. Scrape of a razor.

Joe looked up without raising his head. "You guys hear about the fire last Friday night?"

"That big one north of town? I thought that was Sunday," Jimmy said.

"Not that one," Joe said, although he'd seen it on the TV. "I mean the one behind the place I'm staying. You probably never heard about it because I saw it before it could get going good," Joe said. "If I hadn't seen the flames and sounded the alarm when I did, it would have been big news."

The men had questions, and Joe tried out his firebug theory. "And he'll do it again. But the powers that be didn't believe me. Only this lady fire investigator gave me the time of day. She's an expert, and she got my point." Maybe that was stretching things some, but it wasn't like Maureen was going to pop up and contradict him. "If you've got some random firebug out there, y'all need to be careful."

All in all, he spent forty-five minutes in the barber's chair and left the shop knowing he'd be welcome anytime he passed through town.

"Nice talking to you fellas," he said, and his voice cracked. Maybe they didn't notice—probably didn't—wouldn't want them to think he nearly shed a tear just because they'd been so friendly. All that time alone in the van had made him soft.

As he walked on, Joe thought about Maureen. Maybe he'd stretched a point talking to the guys, but he was pretty sure she had come around to his way of thinking, especially when they both ended up in Littleboro. That proved they were on the same wavelength. It wasn't too bad sitting across the table from her at lunch, either, even if she wasn't his type as far as looks went.

Later in the afternoon, Joe heard the sound of a vacuum cleaner in the hallway outside his room. He stepped out to intercept the cleaning ladies. He'd gotten to know the three of them, a mother, June, and her two daughters, Deb and Linda. All of them were blond and sturdy. The sisters looked like twins. They all dressed alike. Joe could tell June from her daughters because of her age, and because she was the friendliest. They'd been a good audience for his story about the fire too. Something had made him hold back his firebug theory, though. What if they happened to talk to Cubby and let something slip? Joe didn't want Cubby to know he was onto him.

Now it was June pushing the heavy upright vacuum forward and back, a lot like somebody mowing grass.

"Hey, June," he said. "You're not by yourself today, are you?"

June shut off the machine. "No. Linda's cleaning 314 while I do this. You're next."

"That's fine." He was itching to ask questions about the occupant of 314, but it was important not to go too fast, not to be too curious.

"I wish everybody was like you, Mr. Corcoran. You're easy." June's smile was a little crooked, but that made it genuine.

"I told you, call me Joe. How about the guy in 314? Is he easy?"

June frowned. "Now you know, hotel maids have to be like priests. Or doctors." She ran her thumb nail over her lips to zip them. Then she grinned. "I'm teasing you, Joe. The truth is, he used the room three nights during the week last week and left it so clean, it was like nobody was even there. Linda and Deb worked Saturday, and they said it was like a hurricane went through it. Then we found out he had a girlfriend over. Well, I guess they had themselves a fine time."

"I saw her," Joe said, "She looked like a lady."

"Ladies get to have fun, too, don't they?" June leaned on the vacuum cleaner, and maybe she batted her eyelids at him. Could that be?

Joe didn't want June to get the wrong idea. He studied the wall behind her and spotted a blotchy brown stain he hadn't noticed before. "Looks like they need some touch-up paint here."

"I keep telling Terry, but he doesn't do anything unless his uncle who owns the place OKs it, so..." She shrugged.

Something clattered down the hall, and Joe turned to look. Linda emerged from 314 pushing the utility cart loaded with cleaning supplies and extra towels ahead of her. "Mom, you all done with the halls?"

"Almost," June said. "I was telling Joe what you and Deb said about that room on Saturday."

"It was a mess, but we've seen worse." Linda stopped beside her mother. "Terry says he hasn't heard anything else about the fire Friday night. And he said you have a theory, Joe."

Dang Terry, couldn't keep his mouth shut. Joe lowered his voice. "Let's just say, I'm keeping an eye on my neighbor down the hall."

"You're kidding." They said it together. They wanted to know more, so he told his story one more time and added the word "firebug."

"That's why the fire investigator lady asked about telephone books and paper towels," Linda said. "She thinks it was him too."

This was news to Joe. "You talked to Maureen?"

"I don't know her name, but yeah, last Saturday. Can I get into your room now?"

Joe stepped aside. Why hadn't Maureen said anything about talking to Linda and Deb when he saw her in Littleboro? What did telephone books and paper towels have to do with anything?

He went downstairs while the ladies worked, but Terry wasn't at the desk and didn't answer his bell. He went back up and loitered in the hall—June and her vacuum were gone—until Linda came out of his room. Then he took up his seat by the window once more.

Cubby came back a little after five that afternoon. The next day, he once again left early in the morning and returned to the hotel in the late afternoon. Joe concluded even a firebug had to make a living, and Cubby must be doing some kind of business. At least he was spending his nights alone. Maybe the pretty lady was so shocked by what had happened Friday, she'd ditched old Cubby.

But watching the guy go and come, go and come was getting tedious, giving Joe a stiff neck.

Thursday afternoon, Joe had to have a serious conversation with himself. He'd stopped in Raleigh in the first place to get the van serviced. He'd been in town almost a week, and here it was April Fool's Day, and he still hadn't tended to his own business. It meant he'd have to pay Terry for at least a few more nights. The fire and all that had thrown him off track. That and keeping an eye on Cubby. But maybe he'd done all he could, and somebody somewhere out there on the road might need his help.

He asked Terry and got the name of a good garage not a mile from the Highway Home.

"If they can fix me up tomorrow, I'll be on my way soon," Joe said. "Maybe Saturday, Sunday at the latest."

"No hurry on my part," Terry said. "You're a good guest."

22

Maureen had no work on Thursday. It was the first of the month, so people with regular jobs for the state or the city were getting paid that day. She'd worked those jobs, though, and wouldn't trade places, even for a predictable paycheck.

It was late afternoon when the phone rang. She scrambled. "Maureen Boykin."

"Hi, Maureen. It's Dave Shepard from Littleboro. The fire chief."

"Sure, Chief. How are you?"

He cleared his throat. "I'm calling because this morning a town employee went out to a park on the lake to pick up trash and found a little building had burned down. No reason why it should have, so it's suspicious to me. Is that the kind of thing you're interested in?"

"A small random fire? It could be." She twisted the telephone cord around her free hand. "When did you hear about it?"

"Not till a little while ago. The trash collector didn't think it was a big deal since the fire was out, so he waited until he took his lunch break to tell his supervisor. The supervisor got in touch with the lady at parks and rec, and she called me. A big family had reserved two picnic shelters with a grill for a kid's birthday. The parks lady gave me the name and number of the person who made the reservation. I managed to get him on the phone. He said they were packing up to leave—the park closes at sundown—when somebody saw the flames. They used fire extinguishers from the shelters and dipped water out of the lake to put it out. I told him they should have called right away, but he said the fire was out, and the kids were getting fussy, so they went on home."

Maureen listened and thought. The more she'd pondered the hotel fire, the more she was convinced one of the two phone calls that reported it must have come from the firebug. Or, as Joe would have it, from Cubby. Or, since it was a woman who made the call, from the pretty lady with Cubby. They didn't want to burn down the woods, just make a point of some kind. A small fire in a park where people were going to see it right away could have been the same. Somebody wasn't trying to do a lot of damage. Something else motivated them.

"So whoever set the fire picked a place where it would be seen right away, right?" she asked.

"Yeah, but you and I know how fast a fire can spread. It's a stupid risk to take."

"Listen, do you mind if I ride over and take a look?"

"I hoped you would. The mayor heard about it, and he wants somebody to do something. Or look like they're doing something. I can even pay you."

"First thing in the morning then?"

It gave Maureen a rush to think her spur-of-the-moment visit to the chief might have paid off. Could it be the firebug at work? A long shot, sure, but sometimes dots connected.

Maureen went to bed at eleven that night, her regular workweek time, then had to get up and move the alarm clock to the far side of the room because the little electric motor ticked too loud. Was it always like that? Or only on the nights her brain wouldn't shut down until twelve thirty, one?

The alarm went off at 6:45. She and Shepard had agreed to first thing, and fire chiefs tended to be early risers, but still—better not to be too pushy. And the fire itself was long cold and lifeless. That wasn't going to change. She'd aim to get to Littleboro by nine fifteen, nine thirty.

She packed up her equipment, but it was still a little early. She washed her breakfast dishes, drank one more cup of coffee to pass a few minutes. First time all morning, she'd stood still enough to realize something—or somebody—was missing.

She'd gone to Littleboro in the first place because of Joe Corcoran's theory about Cubby being a firebug. The only other person who'd care about the park fire was Joe Corcoran. She called the Highway Home and talked to the boy Terry.

"I'll call his room for you," Terry said.

Maureen had to listen to a few minutes of buzzy silence. It gave her time to decide this was a bad idea. She was about to hang up when Terry came back on the line.

"He's not answering," Terry said. "Don't know where he is. Want me to take your number?"

"He already has it." That was true—she'd given Joe one of her cards. Maybe he'd lost it, so it wouldn't be her fault if he couldn't call back. Or maybe he wouldn't be interested, wouldn't bother anyway.

Right.

23

Joe got to the garage before it opened at seven that Friday morning. The boss unlocked the doors at 6:55 and said, "You may as well come on in."

Joe loved it when things fell into place, little things, big things. His old dad used to say, God's in his heaven, all's right with the world.

Joe explained what the van needed, said he could leave it all day, no problem, and began to walk back to the hotel. He wasn't used to being without his wheels—his home— and it was a lonely feeling.

It was still early when Joe got back to the Highway Home. He went in through the front door, expecting to see Terry behind the desk. Terry wasn't the brightest bulb, but he always looked happy to see Joe and talk a while. Instead, there was a sign with a clock face on it. Both hands were straight up. Back at noon.

Joe took the stairs. Maybe the cleaning ladies would be

working on the third floor. Linda and Deb were always in a hurry, but June made time to visit with him. If he found her that morning, maybe he could get more information about Cubby. Like did they have any idea where he went when he left the room with his briefcase?

But when he got to the third floor, there was no sign of the cleaning ladies. He let himself into his room and smelled the sharp lemony cleaner they used. The carpet showed vacuum cleaner tracks. In the bathroom, two fresh drinking glasses were covered with white paper caps. The toilet had a paper band across the seat. The towels were rolled and stacked in a neat pyramid on the countertop. Nice, but he was disappointed to have missed June or the girls. Like him, they were getting to things early that day.

He hadn't taken time to shower before he went to the garage, so he took a quick one and changed clothes.

Now what? Lunchtime was still a long way off. Where could he get hot dogs as good as the ones he'd had in Littleboro? The chili had been top-notch. Or he could go back to Terry's Chinese place in the strip center next door.

That was when he saw a slip of pink paper tucked under the base of the lamp. He picked it up. He'd missed a phone call. M. Boykin had called him. It took a moment to click. M for Maureen. Well, well.

The night of the fire, he hadn't known how to get an outside phone line and didn't take time to figure it out. Now he squinted at the instructions printed on a card by the phone. Dial 9, wait for the tone, then dial the number. It was going to cost him a little money, but hey, what the heck.

She answered on the fifth ring. "Maureen Boykin." She said it like she was irritated.

"Hey there. Joe Corcoran here."

"I am almost out the door, Joe. The fire captain in Littleboro called me yesterday. A shelter in a town park burned down Wednesday. I'm on my way over there to take a look."

"No kidding?" Once more, fate smiled on him. "My camper van's in the shop. Can you pick me up?"

She sighed loud enough for him to hear. But if she didn't want him to go along, why had she called?

"Fifteen minutes," she said. "Be ready."

24

Maureen started the Wagoneer, tilted the rearview mirror so she stared herself in the eyes: "If he's not out there waiting, I'm not going to stop. I don't have time to wait on Joe Corcoran."

She nodded, agreeing with herself, and drove to the Highway Home.

Just her luck: Joe stood in front of the hotel, wearing his usual khakis, his windbreaker over a plaid shirt, and the red ball cap. He bounced on his toes when she turned into the driveway. OK, he felt the rush too. But would he talk all the way to Littleboro?

The answer was yes, he would.

"Tell me again, word for word. Exactly what did the fire chief say?"

"Joe, I've told you twice. Three times, if you count what

I said on the phone." Maureen slowed down at the Littleboro town limits sign, The Little Town Time Forgot.

He sighed a throaty sigh. "So you know where we're going, right?"

The guy was so annoying. She didn't answer, just followed the directions the fire chief had given her—two clicks around the square, go two miles, turn onto Lakeside Road, and the park would be on her right.

She expected the whole park to be closed off, a crime scene, but no. The gate was open. A dirt road led an eighth of a mile through woods, past a deserted children's playground, and ended at a small lake. It was gray and calm. There was an empty canoe rack—not the season for paddling—with a "for rent" sign hanging off at an angle, a scattering of picnic tables under shelters, some with barbecue grills on concrete posts. They passed a wooden building that looked like it housed maintenance equipment and such.

"There." Joe pointed at a red Ford pickup with a blue light mounted on top. It was parked beside a burned-out structure circled by plastic stanchions and yellow tape.

Maureen saw Dave Shepard leaning against the tailgate and pulled in beside the truck. He was as good-looking as she remembered, and here she was with shlumpy old Joe riding shotgun.

"I'll do the talking, right?" she said. Joe was half out the door before she came to a full stop.

"I was afraid you got lost," Shepard said.

"Sorry. I ran a few minutes late." Maureen offered her hand. "This is Joe Corcoran. An associate." Better be a silent associate.

Shepard shook her hand, then Joe's. "There's not a lot to see, I'm afraid. The folks who put the fire out weren't thinking about preserving the site, and who knows who else has stomped around?"

Maureen nodded. "At least they kept it from spreading. What was this building?"

"Ladies' toilet and dressing room," Shepard said.

It sat on a cement slab. The back half of the roof had collapsed, the front walls scorched but standing.

Maureen pulled on her coveralls and put plastic covers over her boots. She added a hard hat. When she walked to the tape, Joe followed.

"Not you," she said. "We don't want any further contamination."

"But he said it's already—"

She held up a hand, and he hushed.

The scene was well trampled, even now a little muddy from the bucket brigade's work. She walked around a fallen beam and went inside. With the sunlight coming in and her flashlight, she found two scorched places on the floor. Someone had piled up flammable material—plenty of it available all around the building, grass, small branches, dried leaves. In one place, the fire burned itself out without doing any damage.

The second attempt had gotten a grip on the rough-cut paneling and climbed. Not the tight, efficient pattern of kindling plus a splash of something flammable she'd seen at the Highway Home fire. Probably not their firebug. Joe would be disappointed.

She stepped out of the building. Both men were watching her. She crossed the trampled grass to stand with them outside the tape.

"It was deliberate, Chief, but pretty haphazard. I'd say they didn't know much about what they were doing. Did anybody report seeing a suspicious person?"

"The man I talked to said a couple of his relatives saw a car come in late, but he wasn't paying attention." He took a notebook out of his chest pocket and glanced at it. "I gave the police chief my contact's name, and the cops are going to talk to as many family members as they can. What's funny to me is, whoever set the fire didn't wait around long enough to see the fruits of their labor."

"I bet they watched, just from out of sight," Joe said. "They'd want to see it, or why bother?"

Maureen gave him a shut-up look but didn't disagree.

"That's my question," Shepard said.

"You want a formal report from me?" Maureen asked.

"Please, ma'am. Before I left the office to come meet you, I heard from two town council members, all worked up about destruction of public property."

"I'll let them know you're on the job, Chief. I'll take some photos, some measurements, all that."

"Sounds good." He smiled. Good crinkly-eyed smile. "Anything else you need from me?"

Too bad she didn't have a good reason to keep him around.

"I'm all set. I'll be in touch." Maybe deliver the report in person.

There was another round of handshakes, and Shepard departed.

"You said haphazard," Joe said. "I thought our guy was better than that."

"He was." Maureen took her camera out of the car. "It's not the same person."

"Or maybe just tricky, changing things up."

"I doubt it. Sorry. You can look around, just don't go

inside the tape. Maybe there's something outside of the immediate area."

"Yeah, good idea."

She kept an eye on Joe while she got her photos, made her notes, and put her stuff away. He walked along the lake shoreline, stooped from time to time to pick up something, squint at it, then throw it back. She finished up and waved when he looked her way. He trotted over, shrugging, hands spread and empty.

"That's what I expected," she said. "You ready to head home?"

"I was thinking. Maybe we get some lunch before we hit the road."

More time with Joe—not what she planned on, but she was hungry. What the hell? "I could eat something."

"How about that place we went before? I'm going to ask for cheese on my chili dogs this time."

What was he, nine years old? But Maureen caught herself almost smiling.

They lucked into a parking spot on the square, almost in front of the café. The same waitress, Callie, waved them to a table and welcomed them back when she came to take their orders.

While Joe talked hot dog toppings, Maureen studied the menu. Today didn't feel like a chicken salad day. She ordered a grilled pimento cheese sandwich with a side of slaw, iced tea.

"Hey, Callie," Joe called the waitress back. "Do you have a telephone book I could look at?"

"Sure. I'll get it for you."

"What's the phone book for?" Maureen asked when Callie had stepped away.

"I just had a flash of genius. Remember last time she said Cubby's father lived out by a lake? Suppose it's the same lake as the fire. What if we get an address and just swing by there?"

"Why? The fire wasn't set by the same person. You do realize that?"

His flash of genius had lit up his face. Now his cheeks sagged.

"You should never play poker," she said. When Callie put the skinny phone book down and Joe opened it, Maureen leaned across the table to get a look.

"Got a few Tatums," Joe said. "No Quinn. Wait, here's a Bernard Q., Senior. That could be Q for Quinn. And it's on Lakeside Road. That's the road we took to the park, right?" He slapped the page.

"OK, Sherlock. Now what?"

"We eat up and head out there just to scope it out."

Maureen shook her head. "I need to get back to Raleigh. This has already taken more time than I thought it would."

Callie brought their food, and Joe let her take the phone book back.

"Wish I had my wheels," Joe said. "I'd go."

And do what? Well, no danger, at least not today. If he went off on his own tomorrow, she'd be out of it.

25

Joe watched the scenery zoom by on the interstate. Weird how much blurrier everything was from the passenger's seat. Billboards faded. Power poles bent. Exit ramps opened and snapped closed.

"How fast are you going?"

Maureen cut him a look, didn't answer.

He couldn't figure her out. First, she called him, then she didn't want him. Told him not to talk although he could tell she agreed about the firebug not leaving before the flames got going. She liked his lunch idea, didn't mind when he paid for hers—and left a big tip—but wouldn't take a little more time to check out where Cubby lived. What was her deal?

He tried a few subjects for conversation. Had she ever been to Florida? Key West, wow. Did she eat conch fritters? How about Vegas? He hadn't been to Vegas but wanted to go. She'd mentioned poker. Did she gamble?

When they got back to the Highway Home's entrance, he asked, "Could you drop me at the garage up the road? They ought to be done with my camper van by now."

"Where is it?"

"A mile further on. A straight shot."

"That's on my way," she said. "No problem."

When he got out of the car, he said, "Pretty good day, right? I mean, we learned some things."

"It was OK," she said. And then she was gone. He'd meant to ask her what she was doing over the weekend. Oh well. Her loss.

The manager of the garage told Joe the bad news. They couldn't get his new tires from the warehouse until Monday.

Some people might get upset, but it all clicked for Joe. The fire in the park, Maureen's call, now this. Those were signs, he wasn't done in Raleigh after all. He was still there for a reason.

The manager offered Joe a ride to the hotel, but Joe said no. He'd made the walk once that day, didn't mind doing it again. A lot had happened since he left the camper van off that morning. He needed time to let it all settle in his brain.

When he passed by the barbershop, he thought about ducking in for the company but saw through the window they were busy. Three chairs full, a couple of men sitting on the bench. Guys getting a trim before Friday night dates. They'd be taking their wives or girlfriends out to dinner. He kept walking and pondering.

There was an ABC store two doors down from Terry's favorite Chinese place. May as well.

"Hey, how you doing?" Joe said to the clerk. "Fifth of Jack, if you don't mind."

The clerk's smile was weak. "I don't mind." He went down the aisle and came back with the bottle.

"You got a big weekend planned?" Joe counted out his money.

"I work Saturdays."

"Well, you're making people happy, right?"

But the guy was a limp fish. Probably had a clammy handshake. Not somebody to hang around and visit with. Joe tucked the brown paper sack under his arm. He knew one person always ready to chat—Terry. Terry liked egg rolls, so Joe stopped and got half a dozen to go.

He rang the bell at the front desk, and Terry popped out of his apartment right away.

"Hey, hey, Mr. Corcoran. Haven't seen you all day." Terry's grin was goofy but real.

"I've been on the move. You hungry?" He put the Styrofoam box on the desk. The aromas of cooling grease, cabbage, pork, garlic, and ginger rose up when Terry opened it. Joe pulled packets of mustard and duck sauce out of a pocket and tossed them into the box lid.

"Still warm. Nice." Terry tore open a pack of duck sauce and squeezed it over a roll.

"I got a bottle too." Joe waved the paper bag. "If you feel like a little drink."

"My uncle says no drinking on the desk," Terry said.

"Is he here?" Joe looked around like somebody might be sneaking up on him.

"Wait a sec." Terry ate half an egg roll in one bite, then went into his apartment and came back with two glasses. "Just a little."

Joe poured them each two fingers of whiskey and, while Terry finished the egg roll, told him how the camper van wouldn't be ready until Monday and then about the fire in Littleboro, how Maureen had taken him along as her associate, how he'd searched for evidence. "You can guess where my mind went. The firebug. Our friend Cubby, right?"

"Cubby? You mean Mr. Tatum?" Terry took a sip and coughed. He chased it with a bite of egg roll. "How come the fire inspector wanted you?"

"Investigator, not inspector. Don't forget, I'm the one who saw it all go down."

"I don't know, Mr. Corcoran. The fire chief didn't think—"

"I'm wondering, Terry," Joe leaned in and lowered his voice. "You told me you put the long-term people on the third floor. How much longer has Cubby paid for?"

Terry hesitated, like he wasn't sure he should say. He eyed the rest of the egg rolls as if they could be taken away.

"Let me put it this way." Joe sipped his drink. No need to rush. "Has he turned in his key?"

"Last I looked, that room key wasn't in my tray."

That was a no. Good.

"It's Friday night again," Joe said. "We need to be on the lookout." He hadn't thought that until it came out of his mouth. He was the one who'd told Maureen that Cubby would stay far, far away from the scene of the crime. But that had been his head talking, and it turned out to be wrong. It was his gut piping up now. Better listen to the gut.

Terry reached for another packet of duck sauce. "Only a week before the Brave's opening game. Maybe this'll be their year."

Once the boy got started on the sorrows of being a Braves fan, there was no going back to serious business. Joe let him ramble a while, then took the bottle and headed upstairs. He stretched out on the bed and studied the ceiling. Yeah, old Cubby would be back. Maybe he'd have another girlfriend with him. This one wouldn't be so pretty and ladylike. This one would be rougher—Joe remembered what Linda had said about the room on Saturday morning. He didn't like thinking about what had gone on.

It had been a long day. A nap sounded good.

When he woke up, he knew he'd slept longer than he meant to. Long naps made him groggy, that and maybe having that drink earlier than he usually took one. He sat up and pulled the drapes open. Nearly dark. His stomach growled.

And then he saw it: the Caddy in its parking space. See there? Hadn't he said so? Got to trust that gut.

26

Joe wished he'd seen Cubby arrive, wished he knew if he was alone. He picked up the phone and dialed 0.

"Hey, Mr. Corcoran. What can I do for you?" Terry said.

"Did you see him?"

"Who now? Oh, right. Yeah, I did. He and the lady got here about half an hour ago. I was getting a Coke out of the vending machine, and I saw them come in."

Terry wasn't useless after all.

"What did the lady look like?" Joe asked. Not the pretty strawberry blonde. Couldn't be.

"A little old for me." Terry laughed at his own joke, but Joe didn't. "I don't mean she was old, just, you know. She was pretty. Blondish reddish hair. Blue eyes."

"Hmph." Not what Joe wanted to hear.

"Hey," Terry said. "I was about to order some more Chinese. You want something?"

The hot dogs had been a long time ago. "They have sweet and sour pork?"

"Sure. It comes with soup. The wonton's good."

"OK, wonton."

"Want me to call in the order? They deliver. You can pay the guy when he gets here."

And there it was. Buy a guy a few egg rolls, and he thinks you're his wallet. But Joe still needed Terry's eyes and ears. "OK. Call me when the food gets here."

After he hung up, he had another thought. Maybe he should let Maureen know what was going on.

There was no answer. Not home? Or busy? Doing what? He left a message, short and sweet, on her machine. She knew how to get hold of him.

Twenty minutes later, Joe had a chair positioned by the window, a rerun of his first Friday night there, watching and waiting for something to happen. He ate chunks of pork, green pepper, and pineapple while he kept an eye on the Caddy.

The chair got hard on his rear end. Nothing had moved in the parking lot. He turned on the TV. The Rockford Files. Maybe he ought to go to California and find old Jim Rockford—but not till after he got this firebug out of circulation.

He moved to the bed, propped himself up on pillows against the headboard. Every few minutes he craned his neck to see if the Caddy had moved. It hadn't.

He dozed off sometime during Police Woman.

27

After dropping Joe in front of the garage, Maureen gave him one more glance in the rearview mirror, then headed straight home. Another Friday night. Oh well.

The message light on the answering machine blinked at her when she walked in. A phone message from Lucy. "Mo, I need a night out. Cosmic at eight o'clock? No men!"

Whatever Lucy had been up to the week before when she couldn't be bothered to return Maureen's own I-need-a-night-out call, it must have fizzled fast.

The Cosmic Lounge had been their place for girls' nights for more than a decade. It would be quiet that early on a Friday, meaning Lucy was serious about no men. The crowd didn't build up until ten thirty, eleven o'clock.

Maureen studied her closet. Lucy gave her hell about her wardrobe—too many work clothes, seriously outdated going-out clothes—and never going shopping. She could call Lucy and find out what she planned to wear for this man-free evening. Nope. Not giving her the satisfaction.

She found her good black jeans, a black mohair sweater with a bateau neckline, her one gold chain necklace, and gold hoop earrings and spread it all out on the bed. With a full face and poofed hair, she wouldn't embarrass anybody.

Time to shower and scrub the smoky scent from her pores. And eat something before she went out. The Cosmic's food offerings didn't go beyond chips and bar nuts. She would need to have something in her stomach to hang with Lucy.

While she was in the kitchen, she flipped on the TV and caught another report about the industrial park fire. Blaine Autry, the reporter who had been live on the scene days earlier, was in the studio now, talking about the ongoing investigation, expanded to include the ATF, just as Maureen had guessed it would. Autrey seemed to be peeved that he wasn't able to get his questions answered by authorities. He came right up to the point of saying the word "cover-up," then backed off.

"It's early days, Blaine," Maureen said to the screen. She smeared peanut butter on a piece of toast.

When Maureen got to the Cosmic, Lucy's Camaro was already there. Lucy sat at a table just inside the front door. She stood up and hugged Maureen.

"You," Lucy said, "look great. I'm a wreck." She wore leopard print pants, a gold V-neck sweater.

"Cut it out, Lucille. I'm not here to prop up your ego." They both laughed. "I'll get the first round. What do you want?"

Maureen went to the bar and ordered a beer for herself, a piña colada for Lucy.

"Do you want to talk about him?" Maureen set the drinks down and settled into her chair. It was an educated guess that there would be a man behind Lucy's need-a-night.

"Same-old, same-old. Looks good but crashes and burns. Better sooner than later, I guess." She siphoned up a sip of her cocktail with the straw. "Can you believe Sheila is a grandmother?"

"She always has to be first, right? First to get married. First to have a baby."

"Barely in that order." They laughed again.

"Also first divorced." Maureen shook her head. "And remarried before you and I finished college."

"That's what gets me. That second marriage..." Lucy sighed. It was an old lament between them. Only Sheila would bounce back, kid in tow, and marry money. And twenty years later, still be married to it.

"I don't care how much money he has. The man is dull." Maureen took a long sip and relaxed into the alcohol.

"So what's with you?" Lucy abandoned the straw and drank. "You met anybody interesting lately? Fireman? Policeman? Paramedic?" Her eyebrows rose and fell.

That brought Dave Shepard of Littleboro to mind. "As a matter of fact," Maureen said. "But I'm sure he's married. He has a photo of two cute kids on his desk."

"Kids, period? No wife?" Lucy said. "That's encouraging. Tell me more."

Maureen told her about the fire in the park and getting called to investigate. Somehow, she mentioned Joe's name, and Lucy interrupted. "Who the hell is Joe?"

Explaining Joe turned out to be tricky. Nice enough guy, but not like that. A little odd. Lives in a van. No, not homeless, he's got the van. Maureen was careful not to say what she'd sensed when he got out of her car—if she'd given him five more seconds, he'd have asked her out. Not that she would have accepted—no way—but Lucy didn't need to hear all that.

Finally, Lucy went back to the good-looking fireman who might or might not be married. And Maureen had to admit, she made a good point about the lack of a wife in the photo.

Then Lucy finally got down to business, the guy who'd come on strong, then crashed and burned. Where she went wrong, what she had learned. Again. By ten fifteen, the bar was getting loud, the music louder.

"I'm done," Maureen said. "You staying?"

Lucy had an almost-untouched third drink in front of her. She looked puzzled, like abandoning it was something she'd never considered.

"OK," Maureen said, "Call me tomorrow." She gave her friend a little hug and threaded her way through the crowd to fresh air. She wondered when she had lost whatever it was Lucy still clung to. She didn't feel old, not really. She wasn't above a one-nighter, but then again, it had been a while.

Back home, the light on the answering machine was blinking. Ignore it, she told herself. Tomorrow's soon enough. But she couldn't afford to miss a job.

Not a job. Joe Corcoran.

"They're here," he said. "Anything happens, I'll let you know."

"Please don't," she said to the machine and went to bed.

28

Lammie and Cubby were back in bed at the Highway Home. He'd picked her up after work, kissed her right there on the sidewalk where anybody could see, and handed her a single red rose. Countdown complete.

He said, "I want to take you for a nice dinner," and they went to a steak house downtown. They sat in a booth with dark red leather upholstery and high padded sides. The lights were low. The waiters glided and spoke in low voices. A piano player played romantic music.

But neither she nor Cubby wanted to stay long enough to finish the meal. They got the food boxed up and took it with them.

They made love twice, then propped up on pillows, eating bites of steak out of a box with their fingers.

"Guess what I did the other day," Lammie said. "I set my own fire. Just like you."

"You did what?" He sounded like he was afraid to hear the answer.

"I remembered what you said about fire calming you down. I was...I don't know...nervous, I guess. Mama's friend Len was at the house, and I didn't want to talk to them, so I drove around and found something to set fire to."

He raised up to face her. "What was it?" His voice had a tone she hadn't heard before. His eyes were cool.

She pulled the sheet a little higher over her breasts. She'd expected—something different. Was it a mistake to tell him? Too late.

He took the container they held between them and set it on the bedside table without breaking his gaze. "Lammie, I told you, fire's not something to mess around with." His voice got softer. "Why were you so nervous you had to do that?"

It was the perfect question. He cared.

"I took the afternoon off to go shopping." Should she explain it was to buy the things he'd peeled off of her so recently? Should she explain about her drive by the senator's house? And about the senator?

"When I saw Len's truck in the driveway, I decided to drive around." No need to say she drove out to Lakeside Road and went by the entrance to the Tatum's driveway, either.

"You know the park on the lake? The one your daddy gave the land for? I turned in there. The lake was pretty, cold-looking, but peaceful. I wished you were there. Some people were having a cookout, or maybe they had just finished. It was getting late. Then I saw a little wooden building with nobody nearby. I thought about how you said fire calmed you down, and that gave me the idea. Sometimes Mama has a cigarette when she's driving around, so there were matches in the glove compartment." She shrugged and looked up at him.

"You set fire to the little building?"

"It took me two tries, and then it was so pretty, watching the fire climb the wall, I hated to leave."

"Didn't you think what could happen? It could have spread. You could have been trapped. You could have burned down the whole place. The woods and everything."

"You weren't afraid."

He went quiet and pulled back no more than the space created when muscles tighten. Lammie felt the movement, no matter how slight.

"Besides," she said, "I knew those people would put it out."

"But did they? Do you even know? And what if they'd seen you? Lammie, I don't want to lose you." He relaxed and kissed her forehead. "I'm sorry I wasn't there to keep you from feeling nervous."

"It wasn't just Len being at the house. Something reminded me of a man I used to work for. A bad man." She moved closer, and he put his arm around her.

"His name is Senator Harold Wayland." And she spun out the whole story, told him things she'd never told anybody, not even Mama.

As she talked, she laid her right hand on the back of his neck where the constellation of freckles was. Nobody had ever listened to her this way. Or frowned so hard because of how she'd been treated. Cubby's jaw muscles clinched.

"Son of a bitch," he said.

"And now I'm supposed to help with his campaign." She

tried not to cry, but tears leaked out.

Cubby used his thumb to wipe her cheeks. "I'll get us a drink. Stay put."

As if she'd go somewhere. "Hurry back."

The sight of his rear end as he walked across the room almost made her forget everything else. Almost.

He brought two glasses with ice and bourbon. Once he was back in bed, they settled, tapped the rims of the plastic glasses together, kissed, and then sipped.

"The money you told me about," Cubby said. "It's real, right?"

"It's real. I counted it again this week."

"I've got some money too. Savings. And from Dad's estate. Let's take it all, get in the Cadillac, and get the hell out of here."

"Leave Littleboro?"

"I have no reason to stay, except for you. And you would be enough, Lammie. But what holds you here?"

Leave Littleboro, Mama, Attorney Morton, the senator? She felt light all of a sudden. "What about your aunt?"

"I've set things up so she has income from Dad's rental properties. That's why I've been in Raleigh the last few days. And I've told her she can stay in the house as long as she lives or wants to. Her friend Betsy is going to move in."

Leaving Littleboro wasn't a new idea to him. He had it all planned. Had it always included her? Lammie laid her hand on his stomach. "Where would we go?"

"Anywhere you want."

The strange feeling that made her thoughts spin and her body feel soft and weightless—could it be joy?

When Cubby was asleep, she wrapped herself around him, looked out the window into the night. He'd said again he was done with fire. Maybe he was. She squeezed her eyes tight and saw light flickering behind her closed lids. Maybe he'd passed the secret power of flames to her. He just didn't know it yet.

29

Daylight woke Joe. He'd slept in his clothes, his neck cranked to one side. The TV's chipper morning voice told him it was eight-forty. Saturday morning. Friday night was gone.

It took Joe a minute to get the kink out of his neck. Then he looked out the window—yep, the Caddy was still there.

He hated sleeping in his clothes. Everything felt clammy, especially the pants he'd had on for twenty-four hours now. He'd been washing his jockeys in the sink, but he'd worn all the clothes he'd taken out of the van both when he first arrived and since. His clean shirts and chinos were still in it, still at the garage. He'd have to ask Terry if there was a laundromat within walking distance.

He shed everything, added the clothes to a pile on the closet floor, closed the door so he didn't have to see it, and headed to the shower.

The water was hot, the pressure strong. He missed the camper van, missed the road, missed having newness all the time. But clean towels every day, water pounding his shoulders and back, and people to talk to made up for some of that.

The bathroom mirror was dripping steam. He wiped it down and shaved while his beard was soft, wrapped another towel around his waist, and stepped out into the cooler bedroom. Goosebumps all over. Like he had brand new skin.

He wandered to the window, too relaxed to worry—but dang. The Caddy was gone.

Joe grabbed the phone and dialed 0 again. It took Terry a while to answer.

"They gone?" Joe asked.

"Who?"

"You know." Not playing that game again.

"He went to get take-out breakfast from the diner," Terry said. "Asked me if he could bring me something too. Nice guy."

Joe hung up. If Cubby had gone out, was the lady still in the room? By herself? What if she didn't want to be there? What if Cubby had kidnapped her, brought her here against her will? It seemed like the only answer to why a classy lady like her would associate with a scumbag firebug.

It took him thirty seconds to get into the least dirty of his clothes. Another thirty and he was in front of Room 314. The Do Not Disturb sign hung on the knob. He pressed his ear against the door, didn't hear anything. He knocked and called, "Maintenance man." Nothing. "Here to change your lightbulbs."

Not the best line, but he hadn't had time to plan what to say. Did he hear somebody stir inside? Was that a soft voice? What if she couldn't get to the door? What if she was tied up? What if she was afraid Cubby would come back?

He went back to his own room, ripped a sheet of paper off the little notepad by the telephone and wrote: Miss, I am here to help you. Open the door if you can. I am in 312. If you can get to me, I'll protect you. Joe Corcoran. PS-You can trust me.

He glanced at the parking lot. No Caddy. He went back down the hall and slipped the note under the door. Then he knocked again, called, "Look under the door, miss," waited as long as he dared, and ran back to 312 to watch for Cubby to come back.

What if Cubby was the one who found the note? Hadn't thought of that. Cubby had gotten all tough guy on him that one time. It wouldn't happen again. He'd be ready, if he had to be. The heavy flashlight from out of the camper van sat on his bedside table because you never knew when there could be a power outage. Joe hefted it and tapped it on the palm of his left hand. It could do some damage.

30

Lammie watched Cubby get in the car and drive off. He'd be back soon with coffee and food. She had time to straighten the bedding they'd whipped to a froth, take a fast shower, put on one of the lingerie sets he hadn't seen yet. If the food got cold while they made love again, who would care? She thought for a moment she heard a knock at the door, stopped, and listened. Nothing.

She walked naked to the bathroom and was just about to step into the shower when she heard another knock on the door, this time for sure. She knew Cubby had his key with him. Maybe his hands were full.

"Cubby?" she called and started toward the door.

She heard a voice. "Maintenance man."

She froze, ducked back into the bathroom, and closed the door behind her. What was a maintenance man doing this early on a Saturday morning? He wouldn't just come in, would he? She had a robe in the other room, but it was short, barely wrapped around her.

"Here to change your lightbulbs," the man called.

What in the world? The light bulbs were working fine. Something wasn't right.

If she heard a key in the door, she'd scream. That peephole in the door, it didn't work both ways, did it? Could he see her if she stepped out of the bathroom?

She stood frozen, clutching a towel to her chest, her heartbeat thin and fast. No more knocking, no sound of a key. He must be gone. Did she dare get in the shower? Cubby should be back any minute now.

She heard another knock at the door.

"Look under the door, miss," the maintenance man called.

She took a deep breath, opened the bathroom door a crack, and peeked around it. A piece of paper lay on the carpet, just inside the room. When all stayed quiet for a minute, she dared tiptoe across the room and pick it up, read it twice. So strange. What kind of help could she need?

The man in 312. Was that the same man who upset Cubby somehow on their first night at the hotel? What would Cubby do if he saw this note? She'd seen a glimpse of the soldier Cubby when he stared down the man. It scared her a little.

She folded the paper twice and tucked it into the little zippered bag she used for her makeup. Cubby didn't need to know about it.

She showered, put on the fuchsia camisole with a pair of black silk pajama pants, smoothed the bedspread once more, and went to the window in time to see the Caddy pull into its usual spot.

Cubby crossed the parking lot, a cardboard tray with two coffees in one hand, a white paper bag in the other. He looked up—of course he did—and smiled at her. She opened the room door for him and dared sneak a peek down the hall after he stepped past her. Nobody there. The man from 312 wasn't lurking.

They ate sausage and egg biscuits, drank their coffee, lay back on the bed, and whispered. Kids with secrets. Where will we go if—no, when we go? California? Mexico? Did you have to have a passport to go to Mexico? The shoe boxes—how do we get them out of the house without Mama knowing? All that cash—is it safe to drive all over the country with it in the back seat? Maybe Cubby could bolt a steel lock box to the floor of the car trunk.

"I've been thinking about that man," Cubby said. "The senator."

"What are you thinking?"

"That before we go, we should do something to turn his life upside down. The way he treated you—he ought to pay for that."

Lammie stopped breathing. Cubby was thinking about, talking about revenge. When he said out loud that the senator should pay, she thought she might float up from the bed, the roof might open, and she might soar into the sky.

"What will we do?"

"I don't know yet. But I'll take care of it."

In the meantime, they were in their safe place, together.

31

It was early Sunday afternoon when Joe watched Cubby and the lady leave the hotel, get in the car, and drive off. Joe's gut told him, they wouldn't be back that day. Dang. He still didn't know if she got his note.

His stomach growled. He didn't want Chinese again, didn't want to end up buying Terry more egg rolls either.

He set out on foot to find food. He passed a Mexican place, a Hardee's, and finally saw a diner at the far end of the next strip mall. Breakfast all day, the sign said. His eggs were too runny. Toast a shade too dark. He ate it, though. Some days you just had to suck it up.

Back in his room, he sorted out his laundry, rinsed a couple of shirts in the bathtub, and hung them over the shower rod. According to Terry, the closest laundromat was two or three miles away, too far to walk with a sack of dirty clothes. Wash would have to wait until he had his camper van back. He'd get everything clean, stock up on food, and get back on the road.

The road. Sure, he could run through all the reasons he'd stayed at the Highway Home a lot longer than he'd planned. The fire, then another fire. Cubby needing to get taken down. The pretty lady. He'd done what he could for her, hadn't he? And there was Maureen too.

Could he leave with none of those things settled? If he collected his camper van on Monday and drove off, would the loose ends still nag him?

He didn't like that feeling. But maybe the road was the only cure. He spread his Rand McNally Road Atlas out on the bed and turned pages. There were still lots of places he hadn't been. He'd mentioned Vegas to Maureen. He'd head for St. Louis and then decide. It had always been the jumping off point for westward ho, hadn't it?

32

After Lammie got home on Sunday afternoon, she spoke sweetly to Mama, let Len Ogden tell her more about himself over supper on the screened porch, and went to bed early.

She slept deeply. Nothing could touch her, harm her anymore.

Monday morning, she floated to work. All sharp edges blurred in the sweet air. Her neighbors' azaleas were blooming. Colors softened and blended.

When she arrived at the law office, the door was already open, lights on inside. When had Attorney Morton ever beaten her to work? She went in, cautious. Morton's office door was open, and she heard his voice, insistent but low. He was on the telephone. She went to her desk, put her pocketbook away as usual, uncovered her typewriter, and opened the appointment book.

"You promised." Morton's voice got louder and higher pitched. When that happened, he was not in his best state of mind.

Lammie went to stand in his doorway where he could see her. More than once, she'd been able to calm him with a gesture, an upraised hand, palm forward. His wife had whispered that trick to her early on.

He stood behind his desk, holding the phone an inch from his face with his right hand, yelling into it. "You looked me in the eye, and you promised."

He saw Lammie, grabbed a newspaper open on his desk with his left hand, crumpled it, launched it at her. It opened and fluttered to the floor.

She took two steps into the room and picked it up. It was the front page of the Raleigh paper. Headline: Suzette Sutton Announces Run for Statewide Office.

The article began, "Long-time state senator Suzette Sutton has announced she will file to run in the Democratic primary for the office of lieutenant governor. Sutton has been called North Carolina's Gloria Steinem softened by magnolias and moonlight..." It gave Sutton's age—fifty-two—and reviewed her career.

Lammie remembered her well. The senator was in her first term when Lammie began to work in the legislature. Suzette Sutton was much younger than the men who were party leaders, outspoken, always smiling her stretched smile. What drove Wayland crazy was how she somehow got herself front and center in every group photo, how with her blond hair and bright dresses she stood out against the rows of men in their boxy dark suits. But maybe what drove him craziest was how she just walked into his inner office whenever she wanted to, not bothering to knock.

Morton slammed down the receiver. Picked it up and slammed it again.

"Who were you talking to?" Lammie asked.

"That backstabbing, double-dealing state party chairman. They promised us, no primary opponent."

"Oh no." She surprised herself by giving the two words an ironic twist and had to clamp down on a smile. Whenever he wanted to talk politics to her, she denied having any interest. She had not bothered to vote since her time with Senator Wayland, although she didn't tell Morton that. Now she felt a twinge of curiosity. "Is that bad?"

He drooped into his chair. "Of course it's bad, Lammie. Everybody knows, the lieutenant governor is just the governor-in-waiting. And it's his turn. He shouldn't have to waste time on a primary. Especially not against her."

"I see. Should I make coffee?"

"Lots of it. It's going to be a long day." He reached for the telephone.

She closed his door on her way out.

While she waited for the coffee to brew, Lammie let an old memory drift to the surface, an incident in the ladies' room of the legislative building. There was a sitting area with a couch and two chairs known as the lounge, separated from the toilet stalls and sinks by a thin wall. It was universally understood that when two or more women huddled together in the lounge, speaking in low voices, they were not to be seen or heard by the others who came in. It was as close to a private place as they had in that men's kingdom.

One day, Lammie went in to comb her hair and touch up her lipstick before a meeting. Two women sat close together on the couch, one crying, the other talking to her in a low voice, both urgent and soothing. It was Senator Sutton whispering to a tearful girl who worked in the administrative offices. "You'll survive. Hell, you'll thrive. Look at me."

Lammie walked past them and went into a stall to eavesdrop.

"Listen, honey," the senator said, "they are all the same, these men. May their lying, cheating dicks fall off."

Lammie was shocked. She'd never heard a woman use language like that.

"You are not going to quit, not to make his life easier," Senator Sutton said. "You stay till the session is over, show up every day, do your job. Head up, chin out. By then, you will have decided what you really want to do with your life. Then you will get a stellar reference from him. You tell him it's that or else. And just know, your turn will come."

It was a few weeks later that Senator Wayland took Lammie to dinner and told her how he'd always cherish their time together, but...

When she found herself packing to go home to leave Raleigh, she remembered Suzette Sutton's curse: May his lying, cheating dick fall off.

Then she'd gone home and buried it all under her hurt, under Mama's disapproval, under her dreams of the time Cubby would come home, and behind all those shoeboxes collecting money in her secret closet. Now Senator Sutton's name was on the front page of the paper. Now Wayland would know how it felt to be done dirty.

"Lammie." Attorney Morton yelled loud enough for her to hear him in the kitchen. She left the coffee and ran to his office. He had tightened his tie and was pulling on his suit coat.

"Lammie, we have to get in the first strike. We can't wait two weeks to make our formal announcement. She's making hers on Saturday, so it'll be in the Sunday morning papers. We're going to have a gathering of supporters and donors at the senator's house on Friday night. Seven o'clock. You're in charge of invitations. And get the press there. Use that list I gave you."

"Where are you going?"

"To Raleigh. Emergency meeting." And he was gone.

There should have been more time to bask in the warmth of dreams come true. To whisper with Cubby about revenge and escape. To plan. But time was defined now. Four days until Friday.

33

Lammie picked up the telephone and cancelled Attorney Morton's appointments for the day. And the next day too. She found the list of donors and news outlets he had given her. There wouldn't be time to mail invitations. She'd have to make telephone calls. It would take hours.

Instead of getting started, she called the Tatums' house, praying Cubby was home. It was Aunt Dru who answered, said her nephew had told her how helpful Lammie had been with the estate, and yes, he was there.

"Good morning, Lammie." When he came to the phone, his voice was formal. Aunt Dru must be hovering.

"Good morning." She matched his tone. "Would you be available for an early lunch?"

"Certainly," he said. "Eleven o'clock? The Legal Eagle?"

She had an hour and a half. She heard Suzette Sutton's

voice: Do your job. Head up, chin out.

Lammie picked up the list again. She called a few people she knew, people who met with Attorney Morton regularly, and forced a smile into her voice. Yes, so exciting. Yes, the senator's house, Friday, seven o'clock. Of course she'd be there too. Why yes, donations would be accepted. The senator would be so grateful.

At 10:55, she locked the office and crossed the square to the Legal Eagle. Mr. Huey was in his usual place behind the cash register.

"Good Monday morning to you, Lammie. He's in the back."

Cubby had the quietest booth. He stood and smiled at her, held out his hands, pecked her on the cheek. "Hey, sweetheart. You sounded so businesslike on the phone, you kind of worried me."

She slid onto the bench opposite him. "Something has come up." She began explaining—the waitress interrupted, but Cubby waved her away—about Friday night. How important it was. How donors and politicians and TV stations and newspapers would all be there.

"Maybe something could happen to ruin it all," she said.

Cubby's face was in shadow, but the green flecks in his hazel eyes flickered and glowed.

"Is it too soon?" she asked.

"Where does the senator live? I can drive over there this afternoon and scope it out."

She described the house, the yard, the gate. "Do you think you can get in?"

"There's always a way. Give me the address." He pulled a pen out of his pocket and wrote on a napkin. Then he looked for the waitress and waved her over.

"I don't know if I can eat," Lammie said, but she looked at the menu while the girl, Callie, waited. She heard a voice behind her call Cubby's name. His other name.

"Quinn Tatum, is that you?"

Cubby greeted the man, owner of the office supply store on the square, and thanked him for kind words about the late Mr. Bear.

When the man left, Callie said, "Mr. Tatum, my mother says she went to high school with you."

"Lord," Lammie murmured. It would be wonderful to get away from this town. When Callie had identified her mother and Cubby remembered her, Lammie slapped her menu down. "I'll have the vegetable soup and grilled cheese."

"Can I still get breakfast?" Cubby asked. "A western omelet?"

"I'll ask." Callie put her order pad in her apron pocket. "Did your friend find you the other day?"

"What friend was that?"

Lammie studied Cubby's jawline as he tilted his head to talk to the girl. She had traced that jawline with her finger.

"A man," Callie said. "He was with a lady. They came in twice. He was asking where you live and wanted to borrow the phone book."

"Not sure," Cubby said. "Every time I turn around, I'm running into somebody."

"I got the feeling he wasn't from Littleboro. Let me see if the cook will make that omelet for you." Callie walked away.

Lammie peeled the wrapper off a silverware set. Once they left Littleboro, this wouldn't happen anymore, all these people tugging at Cubby. They should have gone someplace else for lunch, someplace where nobody knew them. Or Cubby could have come to the law offices where they could take off their clothes...the couch in Attorney Morton's office...

"Tell me exactly what's the schedule for Friday night?" Cubby said. "You'll be there, right?"

Her mind spun, then got traction. "Attorney Morton can't plan his way out of a paper bag without me."

"Can you put me on the guest list?"

"Of course."

"I'll go to Raleigh this afternoon and figure something out." He put his hand over hers on the tabletop. "You do your planning, and I'll do mine."

"But when will you tell me what's going to happen?"

"Not until the last minute. If you don't know, you can't let anything slip."

He reached across the table and took her hand. They were still sitting that way when Callie slid their plates onto the table. They ate, and Cubby walked her back to the office building.

"Whatever happens Friday night, be ready to leave town right away," he said. "Enjoy your last week in Littleboro."

Attorney Morton blew in mid-afternoon, full of plans. The senator's house was big, but not big enough for the crowd they wanted, so the event would be on the back lawn, even though April nights were cool. The senator's wife was lining up the caterers and rental stuff. Tents, tables, chairs. Musicians. His campaign staff was writing his speech. How was she coming with the guest list? She showed him how many calls she'd already made and promised to work late every night that week.

When Lammie got home from her late nights at the office, she had even more to do, dodging Mama's questions and sneaking supplies—brown wrapping paper, a roll of packing tape, scissors—up to her room. She wrapped and taped up the shoeboxes so they couldn't fly open. Wednesday night, Mama went out with Len, and that gave Lammie the chance she needed to drag her daddy's old footlocker down from the attic and into her secret room. The boxes went into it. She nestled in the envelope with Granny's thirty-four dollars. She folded Granny's wedding-ring quilt and tucked it around the boxes. The footlocker had a hasp for a lock. She'd have to go by the hardware store the next day.

She pondered her clothes and decided she didn't need to pack much. A few dresses for warm weather. Two or three pairs of slacks and matching cotton sweaters. Did they wear those in California? Probably not. She could shop when she got there. Sandals. Loafers. She would leave all her work clothes hanging in the closet. How long would it be before Mama emptied it and discovered the hidden door? She'd find that secret room with its empty shelves and a little girl's stuffed toys and dolls gathering dust.

34

Monday, Joe finally saw his camper van for the first time in three days. The new tires gleamed. The hubcaps too. They made the paint job look even more faded than before. One day, he'd take care of that. For now, he'd settle for a good wash and wax. Inside, he found fingerprints on the dashboard, boot marks on the carpet. A full greasy handprint on the ceiling. Jeez. He didn't mind the guys at the garage sightseeing, admiring his handiwork, but they ought to wash up first.

Before he left town, he'd pull out the mats and shampoo them. Go over the whole interior with soap and a chamois, clean the windows. Find a gas station with a vacuum cleaner by the air hoses. Repack better and tighter than ever. It would take two or three days, but worth it. Get back on the road with pride.

But first, he had to do laundry. If he could have, Joe would have stripped down right there in the laundromat so he could wash every last garment he owned. He hated it that something always had to be dirty. But he was happy inhaling the soapy scent while he sorted and folded clean pants, shirts, shorts, socks.

He stopped at a Western Auto and bought what he needed. He'd seen a hose curled up in the Highway Home's utility room—he'd snuck in to see if he could find brighter light bulbs—and he knew Terry would let him use it. He'd need a ladder to get the top of the camper van. The hotel had to have a ladder. Back when he lived in Florida, before he hit the road, he'd been waxing the van in the driveway, and a nosy neighbor asked him why he bothered shining the roof. "Nobody sees it but the birds." People were so half-assed. It was sad.

By Thursday afternoon, he was done. The van shone, inside and out. The chrome gleamed. His clean clothes were stowed. Fresh sheets on the bed. Canned goods secured. The cooler up in his room was filled. He wondered if the camper van knew, if the highway called to it the way it did him.

He didn't want to head out late in the day. And he'd paid for the night at the hotel. Besides, he hadn't talked to Maureen in almost a week. He should call her to let her know he was leaving. Ask her if she planned to keep an eye on old Cubby. He figured a no was more likely than a yes, and he could see there were problems with the idea. She had to work, after all. Make a living. And she made a good case for the second fire not being connected to the first one, even if he wasn't willing to give up on the idea. But still, he should call.

Back in his room, he picked up the telephone receiver. Chances were, he'd get her answering machine during the day, so he put it down again. He checked the phone book on the nightstand shelf. She was listed, along with her address.

He found Terry at the front desk and asked him if he knew where Cardinal Lane was. Terry pulled out a city map, and together they found it.

"Why're you going there?" Terry asked.

"Just got an errand to do." No need for Terry to know his business. Joe made a sketch of the route. "If I get back in time, I'll get us some Chinese." It wouldn't hurt to treat the kid to one more round of egg rolls.

In twenty minutes or so, he was turning onto Cardinal Lane, a dead-end street in a neighborhood of small houses. Maureen's was light gray with dark gray trim. The grass could use some fertilizer. The shrubs were leggy. Her car was in the driveway.

OK, then. He took a deep breath, got out, took long strides up the walk, and rang the doorbell. He leaned his ear against the door, didn't hear anything, was about to ring the bell again when the door opened.

"Joe," Maureen said. "What...?" She didn't finish the question. "Come on in." She stepped aside.

Joe went in, right into the living room. An upright piano. That was a surprise. A fireplace. Bookshelves with paperbacks and several empty shelves. A small portable TV set. Couch and a pair of chairs.

"You ever use the fireplace?" he asked. Dumb question, maybe, but it seemed logical to ask a fire investigator.

"Too much trouble," she said. "Have a seat."

He took a chair and sat on the edge. She did the same on the couch.

"Sorry to just drop in," he said. "If you hadn't been home, I'd have left a note." He had it written, took it out of his pocket, and offered it.

She unfolded it and read it. Her face scrunched like he'd known it would. "You're leaving town. Going to see more of the country." She folded the note. "That sounds good. Continuing your journey."

"Right." His mouth got sticky. "It's just, I wanted to say bye."

"I appreciate it." She sounded like she meant it.

"And thanks. You know. For taking me seriously. Not many people do."

It was harder to say than he'd expected. His mouth went from dry to flooded, and he had to swallow.

"It's OK, Joe. I mean, you may have been onto something with Cubby, but I don't think we can prove it."

"I know. If we can't prove it, it's like it never happened."

She shrugged and nodded. But she looked sad. He stood, and so did she. At the door, he didn't know what to do and was glad she did. She stuck out her hand, and he shook it, both of them with stiff arms.

"Maybe you can send me a postcard or two," she said.

"Yeah, I'll do that."

Back in the van, he felt his chest rise and fall, rise and fall. Deep breaths.

He got a little lost on his way back to the Highway Home. Traffic was heavy, and he was in the wrong lane to make a left turn. But he was good at finding his path again. Lots of practice. Part of life on the road.

He pulled into his parking space near the dumpster. The Caddy was in its place too.

35

Joe went in through the back door. He checked the elevator, something he always did now. It was there, ground floor. He headed for the reception desk. See what Terry knew. He slowed down when he heard a man's voice, then Terry's saying "un-huh, un-huh." Joe sucked in his stomach and went down the hall to the lobby. Yep, it was Cubby talking, his back to Joe, saying "...one more night, tomorrow night."

"OK, Mr. Tatum. Since you been such a good customer, I can give you a discount on the extra night." Terry fiddled with his registration book. When he looked up, he saw Joe. "Hey, Mr. Corcoran. Be right with you."

Cubby turned. Joe hadn't been close to him since that first night, when Cubby got up in his face. Acted the big man. All that.

Now Cubby didn't seem to register who Joe was, just went back to paying Terry. Maybe when he went by, he came a little closer to Joe's shoulder than he had to. Maybe he smirked. Then he was gone. Joe heard the elevator ding.

"You thinking about Chinese?" Terry asked Joe. "Your last night here." He said it like it made him sad.

"I may need to stay one more night," Joe said. "You going to give me the discount too?"

"Sure. I got used to you and Mr. Tatum being around here. Only bad thing about my job—I get to know somebody, and they take off."

Joe nodded and reached for his wallet.

Joe sat in his window and ate General Tso's chicken. Too much broccoli. He always wondered if they even had broccoli in China. At least there was lots of sauce. He let the rice soak it up while he watched the parking lot. In a while, Cubby came out the back door, got in the car, left. What about his lady friend? Was she in the room?

Joe saw the light from his own room laid a patch on the pavement below. No matching patch from 314. Somehow, he just knew she wasn't there. He'd sense it if she was. What was old Cubby up to?

He finished his food and went downstairs, just for something to do. He unlocked the van and got in, gripped the steering wheel, and settled his rear end into the seat. When he drove it from the garage, he noticed the new tires were noisy, but they'd ride good.

For the heck of it, he pulled out of the parking space, turned the van around, and backed in. Ready for a quick getaway. But not tomorrow morning after all. Could still change his mind and go. Except he'd paid for the extra night. He doubted Terry's uncle let him give refunds.

Headlights swung around the corner of the building, and Joe slumped down. The lights cut out before they reached him, though. He raised his head to see the Caddy back in its place and Cubby crossing toward the hotel, carrying what looked like a toolbox. Heavy, from the way he leaned to balance. Something was going on.

Joe had seen a lot of cop shows. Stakeouts were always boring. Guys in the unmarked cars drank a lot of coffee and ate a lot of junk food. But there was always a big payoff. That's what Joe counted on all day Friday, with nothing to do but keep track of Cubby. A payoff. The guy went out early. Came back. Opened the trunk and acted like he was rearranging stuff. Left again.

Joe ate Slim Jims he'd bought the day before, drank a Coke from the machine downstairs, chatted with the cleaning ladies who said they heard he was leaving.

June said, "We wish all the guests were like you, Joe. You make our job easy. And you talk to us like we're people, not like we're the maids."

"Not like some people," Linda said.

Was it Joe's imagination or did she point her chin toward 314?

"You ladies do a great job," Joe said. "If anybody gives you a hard time, shame on them." He hoped they'd say more about Cubby, but Linda fired up the vacuum cleaner.

June lingered a minute. "Reckon you'll ever come back?" She smiled.

Joe felt his eyes widen and his mouth twitch. Like Maureen said, he had no poker face. "Maybe. Who knows?" That wasn't a question he'd ever asked himself.

It was half past three when the Caddy returned. This time, the pretty lady was with Cubby. He opened the trunk, and they both stood looking in. They talked, their heads together, and she leaned against him for a moment. They kissed and then headed inside, carrying a garment bag and a little suitcase.

Joe had to accept it. The pretty lady was a real disappointment, but he'd done all he could do with the note and the offer to help. He'd even been ready to wield his flashlight if he had to. Well, if this was their last night at the Highway Home, and his, too, then there wasn't much more to say.

All Cubby's comings and goings still made no sense to Joe. Something else he'd have to live with. He heard the elevator ding on the third floor. He didn't have anything better to do—may as well keep watching.

When Cubby and the lady came out again more than an hour later, they'd changed clothes. She was wearing a black dress and fancy shoes. Cubby was in a suit and tie. Going somewhere special then. What if he followed them? Joe grabbed his keys and ran down the stairs the way he had the night of the fire, so fast he missed a few steps but stayed on his feet.

The Caddy was backing out, turning around when he got to the camper van. Smartest thing he'd done in a long time, park facing out, ready to go. He had to be careful now, though. The camper van wasn't exactly going to blend in with traffic. Couldn't trail them too close. He'd learned that from cop shows too. He eased around to the front of the building in time to see the Caddy make a left turn.

They got separated at a traffic light, but Joe caught up at the next one, with a few cars in between for camouflage. All three of those cars turned off suddenly in the next block, so if Cubby glanced in the rearview, he'd see the camper van. Would he recognize it from the Highway Home?

Joe slowed down and let a couple of impatient people go around him. Cat and mouse, cat and mouse. He broke into a light sweat.

36

Maureen was up early Friday morning, went for a run, and was slugging OJ out of the carton when her phone rang. Who called at eight fifteen? She hoped it wasn't the insurance company that wanted her to check out a scene in a Rocky Mount warehouse that day. They'd only call to cancel.

"Maureen Boykin."

"Hi, Maureen." A male voice. Familiar but not quite... "Hope it's not too early to call. This is Dave Shepard from Littleboro." He paused, giving her space to remember. As if she needed to think twice.

"Chief, hi. Any problem with my report?"

"No. It was fine. Thanks." Another pause. "Listen, I'm going to be in Raleigh today, wondered if maybe you could meet with me in the afternoon."

Her fingers seemed to want to drop the phone. She gripped it between her shoulder and chin. "I've got a job today—" No, no, no. Don't say no, idiot. "But I can be back by five. Is that too late?"

"Actually, that'd be good. Here's the thing." He cleared his throat. "I'm interviewing for a job with the Raleigh Fire Department. I was thinking you might know a lot of those guys. Maybe you could, you know, give me a little advice."

Very interesting.

"I could probably tell you a thing or two about the department. As long as it's just between us, you know?"

"Yeah, of course, great. I know you're likely to have plans, but any chance of getting something to eat while we talk?"

"I can do that." Keep voice neutral. "You need to get back to Littleboro by any certain time?"

"My ex has the kids this weekend, so no worries. You want to suggest a place?"

The ex had the kids. Lucy was right.

"Sure. I know a place, not fancy but good. Let me get the exact address." She grabbed the phone book, found the listing, and read the address off to him. They agreed to meet there at six o'clock.

Maureen was later than she meant to be leaving Rocky Mount and got home on a prayer that the highway patrol had better things to do than pull her over for speeding. She took a quick shower and pondered her wardrobe. She wanted to look good, but not like she was trying too hard. Her black jeans, a plain white T-shirt, her dark brown leather jacket, and boots that almost matched. Gold necklace and hoop earrings. Makeup. Hair? Ugh. Loose would have to do.

She got to the restaurant at 5:55 and saw Shepard's red truck with the Littleboro Fire Department insignia on the side. She parked, flipped down the sun visor to check herself in the mirror. Added a layer of lipstick, inhaled, exhaled, got out of the car, and headed toward the front door. Funny, she thought. Third time in what—two weeks?—she'd been out to eat with a man, but definitely not on a date. Right?

She saw Shepard at a table by the window in the bar. He stood up as she approached. Lucy would have a fit if she saw him, he looked so good. He wore what passed for a dress uniform for a small-town fire chief. Dark brown pants, the crease still sharp at the end of the day, a tan shirt, starchy collar. He'd probably had a tie on earlier, but now the shirt collar was open. He grinned and held out his hand.

"Thanks for coming, Maureen. How's your day?"

"Not bad. How was yours?"

"Yeah, I think it went pretty well. They said they'd get back to me by early next week."

"That's great. Good for you."

"You hungry? Are the wings any good?"

They got a couple of beers and an order of wings.

"Double major in chemistry and physics, huh?" Shepard asked.

When she quit choking on a swallow of beer, Maureen managed, "You read my resumé?"

"Wasn't I supposed to?" Dave Shepard had a truly great grin.

Maureen had met a lot of firemen in her life, but they either hit on her or treated her like a useful oddity, or both. Once she established she wasn't interested in anything but the job, that was it. This guy was different.

The round of beer and chicken wings was followed by another beer each, cheeseburgers, and fries. Dave carried pictures of his kids but didn't get them out until Maureen asked.

"They're pretty average, I guess, but I'm crazy about them," he said. The look on his face told her, he thought they were anything but average. There was no talk about the ex except to say, she was a good mom.

A nice change from most divorced men whose exes were all crazy, if not bat-shit crazy. Maureen always wanted to say, maybe you're the one who made her crazy. And Dave was funny, full of stories about just how little Littleboro was. She thought about Joe and asked the question she knew he would have: did he know a man named Quinn Tatum? Dave did not. OK, Joe, duty done.

They talked about Raleigh as a place to live. She began to think—hope—the evening wouldn't end the minute the check came. Another beer? Why not? Here's to Friday.

Dave turned his head away, like something outside got his attention. Then she heard it—a siren, no, a lot of sirens. Cars passing by the restaurant pulled to the side, and one, two, three firetrucks went past at speed. She and Dave looked at each other.

"Want to go to a fire?" he asked.

37

Friday morning, Lammie told Attorney Morton she needed time off to get her hair done.

"You want me looking my best when I greet all those important people," she said, and her boss beamed at her.

"We make a good team, Lammie. I'm thinking I should run for office myself. You'll be my gal Friday. You're too good for Littleboro anyway."

Nice of him to notice. She covered her typewriter and gave it a pat. What if, next time somebody turned it on, it automatically typed out Lammie Timmons's life story? Nobody would ever have guessed she'd go out in a blaze of glory one day.

She took her purse out of the drawer and smiled at the empty space it left. She picked up her brass nameplate, dropped it in, and closed the drawer. Mary Lambert Timmons was gone.

Marie's Beauty Box did steady business on Fridays. Everybody getting pretty for the weekend.

Marie dug her fingers into Lammie's scalp under soft running water. "This isn't your regular day, Lammie. You got something special planned?"

Lammie lifted her hand out from under the plastic cape to wipe a drip off her cheek. "A big political event in Raleigh tonight."

"My, my. Didn't know you were political." She wrapped a towel around Lammie's head and raised her up.

"We're hoping the governor will drop in." That wasn't true. The governor had made clear he would not endorse either of the primary candidates, but Marie was more likely to make this a topic of conversation the rest of the day if the governor was involved.

"Let's make you look extra nice then," Marie said. "Your mama has her usual appointment this afternoon. Is she going to be at this shindig?"

"No, I'm sorry to say." Lammie checked her sad expression in the mirror, lips tipped down, eyes wide and almost liquid. Then she brightened. "You know she has a new man in her life?"

"Miss Mary Ruth has a beau? She's been keeping secrets from me. Do tell."

Lammie imagined the conversation Marie and Mama would have that afternoon. It would irritate Mama to realize Marie knew more about Lammie's life than she did, and now her big announcement about Len Ogden would be preempted too. Mama would be in a fine snit by the time she got home, but Lammie wouldn't be there for it. Ha.

Lammie wanted to be out of the shop, on to the rest of her life, but Marie would not be hurried. There were hair rollers, time under the dryer, the combing out of tight sausage-shaped ringlets into a pile of soft curls, a fog of hairspray.

Finally, Marie studied her in the mirror, used the tail of a rattail comb to add a little lift to Lammie's hair, fixed it with one more puff of spray. "You will be the prettiest lady there. Be sure you mention, hair by Marie."

Cubby and the Cadillac were waiting outside the salon. Lammie slid into the car, leaned over, kissed him. At her house, the driveway was empty as expected. Friday mornings, Mama made the rounds of businesses she did bookkeeping for, dropped off whatever work she'd done for them that week, and left her invoice. She had lunch with her lady friends and went to have her hair done.

Lammie had not said anything about her plans to Mama except that, once again, she would be gone all weekend. They had locked eyes, and it was Mama who looked away. Was that a blush on her cheeks? Maybe with her own new sweetheart, she was happy enough for Lammie to clear out of the house.

It took twenty minutes for Lammie and Cubby to move her suitcases and the footlocker to the car. No doubt Miss Leora was watching. Another thing happening for the last time.

It would be Miss Leora who told Mama her daughter and Quinn Tatum looked like they were taking everything they could carry out of the house. Yet Mama wouldn't be able to tell anything was gone other than a few clothes.

And by the time Mama got seated in Marie's chair, Lammie and Cubby would be halfway to Raleigh and the Highway Home.

Lammie gave a little laugh, and Cubby said, "What's funny?"

"I'm just happy."

They did not talk on the drive, did not need to. Lammie lapped up the silence. Her life rode on the smooth tires, the purring engine of the Caddy, glided toward the future. She closed her eyes, put her hand against the window, her cheek against her hand, and felt the big car's vibrations through the cool glass.

"Hey, sleepy head." Cubby touched her shoulder.

She sat up, lost for a moment, then saw where they were. Their parking space behind the hotel, the trees still charred from their first night together there. She'd not even known about the power of fire, not until that night. "What time is it?"

"We're fine," Cubby said. "We don't have to hurry."

"But I need to shower, dress, do my makeup, get to the senator's by five."

"We have a minute." He shifted to face her. "We could back out of here right now and head west. We could get into Tennessee by dark."

"You mean you don't want to do it—what we planned?"

"It's all about you, Lammie." His eyes were steady on hers. "If we do it, it's for you. If we don't, it's for you."

The momentary panic released its grip. She thought about how helpless Attorney Morton and the senator would be if she didn't show up. Neither one of them would have a clue what to do without her. That was a little bit of revenge. But not enough.

She could only whisper, "We do it."

38

"Last time," Cubby said. He held the door of 314 open for her. "You going to miss it?"

"I will," she said. "It's our safe place." She leaned against him for a moment.

Cubby was businesslike. He set down the bag he carried. "Let's sit down, and I'll tell you what's going to happen." They sat opposite each other at the dinette.

"An alley runs behind the senator's house," he said. "It's open to the side streets at both ends. The whole property is fenced in, with a cattle gate at the back on the alley. They probably open it to put out the trash cans, use it for deliveries so they don't have all those trucks coming in the front gate. They have that electronic gate at the front of the house, but anybody could climb over the gate at the back. They may as well not have any security at all."

"You've been inside the fence? What if somebody had seen you?"

He laughed. "Sweetheart, these people live in a bubble. They are begging to have it popped."

His eyes were all she could see, bright and unblinking while he talked. He exhaled strength, and she inhaled it.

"There's a garden shed," he said. "It's supposed to look like a fairytale cottage, I guess. Do you know what's inside a garden shed?"

She tried to think what was in Daddy's shed in the backyard at her house. "Lawn mower. Clippers. Old flowerpots."

"All that," Cubby said, "and gas cans. Fertilizer. Bales of pine straw. I won't have to bring anything in, just use what's there."

"You said you were done with fire."

"I know. I'm making an exception, and I swear this will be the last one."

He was breaking his oath, for her. Setting the world on fire one more time, for her.

"Will it be dangerous?"

He explained—a timer, a small explosion, a safe distance from the house, nobody hurt, only the shed and what was in it, but plenty of disruption, chaos, ruin the senator's big moment—but she could barely take in what he said. She imagined flames reaching to the heavens. She could see it, smell it, hear it.

"Are you listening?" he said.

She shook herself out of the trance. "Yes."

"Repeat it back to me. Where are you going to be? What are you going to do? Where are you going to go?"

"I'll be out of the crowd, by a phone. I'll call 911. Then I don't run. Other people will run, but I don't. I walk down the drive, out through the front gate. I turn right. You'll be at the end of the block with the car, waiting."

"OK. One last decision. What time do we want it to go off?"

"People start coming at six. I stand on the front porch to greet them, check their names off the list, tell them to go through to the backyard. They get something to eat, something to drink. There'll be music. At seven, Attorney Morton will introduce the senator for his big speech."

"Will he be on time?"

"The senator was always a stickler about his schedule." He wanted her always to arrive for their dates before he did. Once, she'd been late. He'd been mean—made her cry.

"Then we'll make it ten past seven. Give me your watch."

She took it off and handed it to him. He looked at his own and adjusted the time on hers. She put it back on. They'd always be together this way.

She changed into the black dress she'd worn to Mr. Bear's funeral. She touched her hair. She and Cubby hadn't made love—that was for later—so the pouf Marie had sprayed in place wasn't disturbed. Taupe eye shadow, black liner and mascara, pink lipstick and cheeks. She wished she'd brought the red instead. After tonight, she'd only wear red lipstick.

When she stepped out of the bathroom, she found Cubby sitting on the bed. He had put on a midnight blue suit, a starched white shirt, a flowered tie.

She held her arms out from her sides, did a pirouette. "Do I look like a mad bomber?"

"Perfect disguise. Nobody would believe it." He stood up and put his hands on her shoulders. "You're going to be fine." He kissed her forehead. "Time to go."

"Let me get my shoes." She had black pumps with a low chunky heel, shoes she could walk fast in if need be. She wouldn't carry much, just her tote bag with the clipboard in it, her small satin purse with the shoulder strap, and her black bouclé jacket in case the evening was chilly.

Cubby left the room key on the table and pulled the door closed behind them.

39

When the senator's gate opened for the caterer's van, Cubby pulled in behind it. The caterers veered off on a narrow dirt track that went to the back of the house. Cubby stayed on the main drive and stopped at the front steps. A man in a red jacket appeared at his window. "I'll have a valet park your car, sir."

"No need. I'm just delivering the lady."

Lammie opened her door, and the man in red was there to offer her a hand. She turned back to Cubby, needing one more smile.

"I'll be back here by six," he said.

She accepted the man's hand, slipped out of the car, and planted her feet. She didn't turn to watch Cubby drive off but felt the empty space he left. The red-coated man disappeared. The wide front steps were steeper than she had remembered. She held the railing and climbed them slowly. The front door opened, and Attorney Morton came out.

"Lammie, right on time." He gave her a peck on the cheek. Had he ever done that before? Maybe when she went through the receiving line at his daughter's wedding. "You ready?"

She smiled and raised the clipboard.

"Lyle," a man called from inside. And then Senator Wayland himself stepped out of the house.

Lammie had not seen him in years. She'd been preparing herself. Hearing Suzette Sutton's voice. Survive and thrive. Get on with your life. Lying, cheating dicks.

Had he been preparing to see her? He'd always kept his facial expressions controlled, but she hoped for something. There was no recognition in his eyes. Nothing.

She'd seen him on TV and in pictures over the years. He was close to sixty now. Thicker in the neck, in the middle. Hair still full, mostly gray. Coarser looking. It photographed well.

"Hal," Attorney Morton said, "you remember Lammie Timmons. She's my right hand—used to work for you."

A flicker. She wanted to think there was a flicker. "Yes. Miss Timmons. Nice to see you again. Lyle says he can't do without you. Lyle, I'm still tinkering with my speech. Come tell me what you think." He took Morton by the elbow and steered him back into the house.

Lammie followed. A massive flower arrangement stood in the middle of a round table on a Persian rug in the entry hall. Double glass doors to the right led to a formal living room with upholstered furniture. Matching doors to the left opened to a library with dark paneling and floor-to-ceiling bookcases. The central staircase was carpeted in dark blue.

The two men left Lammie and walked down a hallway to the right of the staircase. They were deep in conversation before they were out of sight.

"Hal? Harold? Where are you?" A voice from above.

Lammie looked up. A woman stood at the head of the stairs wearing a long pink robe. She had pink foam rollers in her hair, and her right arm was in a sling. Lammie had only seen Mrs. Wayland once or twice before, but she recognized her. Mrs. Senator, the older secretary always called her.

"Oh," Mrs. Wayland said when she saw Lammie. "You'll do. Come up here."

Lammie put her hand on her chest. Me? But the woman had disappeared. So Lammie went up. A bedroom door stood open at the head of the stairs. Mrs. Wayland waited for her and closed the door behind her.

"Today of all days. I cracked my elbow. Couldn't get to the hairdresser. My daughter put these rollers in, but she had to pick up her children." She sat down at a dressing table. "Get these things out of my hair."

Then she sighed. "I apologize. I don't know you, do I? Would you please be so kind?" She gestured with her left hand. "Please." She eased the sling off and laid it across her knees. Her right arm was heavily bandaged, the elbow immobilized at an angle.

Lammie stood behind her and began to loosen the rollers. "I used to do this for my mother. When I was little." The woman's eyes met hers in the mirror. Was Lammie saying Mrs. Wayland was old enough to be her mother? Yes, she was.

"Hand me the brush," Lammie said. She was gentle as she smoothed out the woman's hair.

"You can just pull it back and use this clip." The clip was a gold oval with diamond chips all around. Mrs. Wayland's hair, dyed dark, was just long enough to gather at the nape of her neck and stay in place. She already wore diamond stud earrings the size of large peas.

"Give it a spray to keep it from frizzing," Mrs. Wayland said.

Lammie used the hairspray lightly, just as Marie had done to her. She glanced at her watch. Five thirty. "I do have to get back downstairs. I'm supposed to check people in as they arrive." What would Cubby think if he couldn't find her?

"Just a minute." Mrs. Wayland shed the robe and pointed to an emerald green dress lying on the bed. "If you can hold it for me, I can step into it. You'll have to zip it." She wore a black lace-trimmed slip Lammie envied. "My husband was supposed to help me. Useless man. Thinks he can run the state, but—Sometimes, I think I might vote for Suzette just to spite him."

Lammie smiled. Me too. But I won't be here on election day. I'll be far away.

She zipped the dress. The expensive fabric draped in all the right places. Mrs. Wayland was tall. And wide. Lammie remembered how she'd sweep into the office, not pausing to say good morning, or kiss my foot. An expression of Mama's. It made Lammie smile again.

"One more thing," Mrs. Wayland said. "Help me get the sling back on."

They managed without disturbing hair or jewelry. "Thank you, dear." Mrs. Wayland's thanks came out a croak.

"I'd better go," Lammie said. "They'll be looking for me." But she didn't hurry out. She took in the room—large bed with a pale blue satin spread, flowered drapes around the floor-to-ceiling window, held back by tasseled swags. Soft chairs covered in soft colors. A fireplace with logs perfectly laid, but Lammie guessed they were never lit. She glanced out the big window. It overlooked the back lawn where three men were setting out white folding chairs, all the way to the flower borders against the fence. It could have been for a garden wedding. And the garden shed, just as Cubby had described it. A person could see everything from that window.

Lammie left Mrs. Wayland leaning into the makeup mirror for one last dab of a brush.

"Where have you been?" Attorney Morton met Lammie at the foot of the stairs. "You need to see the setup."

He took her arm and steered her down the hallway. They passed a dining room and the kitchen and went out through a French door. The flagstone patio was covered by a blue-and-white-striped awning. Beyond it, the lawn was the rich green of Mrs. Wayland's dress, even this time of year. Ladies would have trouble with their high heels in the plush grass.

Lammie looked past the rows of white chairs, past the banks of azaleas bordering the lawn, to the garden shed. It was shingled, painted white with red gingerbread trim. Red shutters on the windows. A fairytale cottage. And a safe distance from the house. Just as Cubby said.

"The bar's over there." Morton pointed to the right. "And the caterer's over there."

The bartenders and waiters clustered under their tents, nothing to do yet. They were like puppets with no puppeteer. Only the food prep people were busy, bringing out covered pans, lighting Sterno cans.

Morton kept talking. "You tell people to come through the house and out here. They can get something to drink and eat, get them in a giving mood." He cackled. "And the reporters. You send them around the side of the house. I'll be watching for them, and Harold can give them a quick interview before he makes his speech. This is going to be a great night, Lammie."

"Yes, it is."

"And I've made sure Harold knows you did a fine job with the invitations. He's very pleased."

40

The first car arrived at straight-up six o'clock, and Lammie was on the front porch, ready with her smile and clipboard.

The man in the red jacket had reappeared with two young men in red vests. The man in the jacket was the boss. He opened car doors for ladies, took keys from men, then handed them to the boys who drove the cars away and came running back to do it again.

Lammie welcomed the guests, checked their names against her clipboard, pointed the way through the house, and turned to greet the next group. She smiled even as she kept people moving when they wanted to clog the doorway and chatter.

At one point, there was a lull, and the red-jacketed man looked Lammie's way. He gave her a thumbs-up. "Good job, miss."

She wiggled her fingers in a wave. These men. Throwing their crumbs of praise.

Then she saw Cubby strolling up the driveway, looking all around, stepping aside for a car to pass him. He looked like he might be a big donor, as big as any of the mill owners and bankers on her list. He paused to speak to the valets, joking about no car, maybe he'd tip them anyway, then turned and fixed his gaze on Lammie. She'd never get used to it—how that look took her in. No crumbs from this man.

He kissed her cheek, just a brush of lips, enough to make her shiver, and then went inside. She composed herself for the next arrivals now getting out of their car.

At five minutes before seven, every name was checked off the list.

"That's all," Lammie called to the red-jacket man. He signaled his workers, and they disappeared around the side of the house.

Lammie went inside and stood in the foyer, taking it all in. Not just the furnishings and flowers, but the sensations of the last two hours. It was the last time in her life she'd have to nod and smile and zip up dresses for women who told her she would do and then croaked their thanks. The last time she'd do the bidding of men like Morton and Wayland.

Seven o'clock. She was supposed to be near a telephone, someplace where she wouldn't get caught up in the crowd. She'd seen a phone in the library and a phone in the hallway just outside the kitchen, but the one she felt drawn to was the one beside Mrs. Wayland's bed. That bed. Did the senator sleep in it too? Did that smooth-as-glass spread ever get yanked off, dropped on the floor, or wrapped around two naked bodies? Not likely. And the way he snored—she hadn't thought of that in years—Mrs. Wayland wouldn't put up with that. No, the important man slept in some pokey little room all by himself.

She went upstairs and into the bedroom, straight to the window. She looked down onto the blue and white canopy set up over the patio. It blocked her view of the podium where the senator would make his big announcement, but beyond it, she could see the bar, the food tables, people making their way onto the lawn, filling the rows of white chairs. And she could see the garden shed.

She opened the window a few inches and heard the trio providing music for the cocktail hour break into "Happy Days Are Here Again." That had been Morton's idea, and she'd told him it was wonderful. But really, Wayland was FDR? Her grandmother, the one who taught her about money, had loved FDR.

The music stopped. Someone tried to get a chant going, "Way-land, Way-land," but it fizzled. The microphone squealed.

Cubby was out there, even though she couldn't see him.

The microphone squealed again, and Attorney Morton called the crowd to order. "Friends, supporters, welcome."

The countdown was on. Her eyes were on the garden shed, but somehow, that wasn't enough. It wasn't enough to wait for Cubby. She wanted to do something too. She needed to leave her own mark. But what?

The lipstick Mrs. Wayland had used lay on the dressing table. Lammie could steal it. Or she could use it to write a message on the mirror. But there were other lipsticks. Mirrors could be cleaned. What else?

Applause rose and fell. Morton was done. The senator took over. His baritone rolled out thanks, welcomes, gobbledygook. It was ten past seven.

Across the lawn, at the edge of the property, the garden cottage shimmered like a mirage, then burst into flames.

The explosion wasn't as loud as she expected. Nor had she expected the windowpanes to vibrate when the wave of sound hit them. Lammie jumped backward. She held her breath, reached out her hand to touch the glass, to be sure it was still solid, then stepped forward again.

The speechifying stopped. The screaming started. People began to run in all directions. Some men ran toward the fire, but others yelled, "get back, get back," and they stopped, turned like a flock of birds that can only move together, and ran the other way.

Mrs. Wayland in her emerald dress huddled in the middle of the yard, her good arm clutching her injured one. She turned toward the house and looked up. Straight at her bedroom window. She opened her mouth in a scream.

Lammie didn't pull back. Another window, another view of a world coming apart. Another person staring up at her, not seeing her, but staring.

She shook herself. She had to make the phone call. She lifted the receiver on the bedside phone and dialed. Say explosion, fire, hurry, hurry, and hang up, Cubby had said. Then she had to go, walk down the driveway. Cubby would meet her on the corner.

But first, she had to make her mark.

A long, narrow brass box on the mantel held matches. The can of hairspray was already uncapped.

41

Joe tailed the Caddy from the Highway Home until it turned into a driveway in a fancy neighborhood. He slowed down, then glided by. He saw the wall, the gate, the long drive. There must be a house back there.

He found a side street a block away with on-street parking, left the van, and trotted back. Now some young guy in a red vest stood by the gate.

"What's going on?" Joe asked, just a friendly passerby.

"Private party, that's all I know. I make sure anybody coming in is on the list."

"Big shots, huh?"

"Politicians. This town is full of 'em. Invitation only. You'd think it was the freaking White House."

Joe wanted to linger. "You get paid pretty well for standing here?"

"I'll be valeting cars later. Minimum wage, but the tips are usually OK."

And boom, just like that, the Caddy reappeared, coming out maybe fifty feet away. So the driveway must make a loop. Joe got a good enough look to see Cubby was alone in the car. He'd dropped the pretty lady off. Now how did those two get invited to a party like this one?

"Good luck," Joe called over his shoulder to the boy in the vest. He picked up his trot, following the car again. If Cubby accelerated, Joe would lose him, and if he tried to get the van, he'd lose him for sure.

But Cubby didn't go far. There was a church with a big parking lot, and he pulled in there. Joe had a hunch. He ducked behind a hedge and waited. Another stakeout, and Joe's gut said there'd be a payoff. Sure enough, in a while, here came Cubby, walking back in the direction of the house.

42

Joe waited in the hedge by the church for a while, but his legs cramped, so he took a chance and walked back toward the party house one more time. Now cars were going in pretty steady, coming out the other end of the loop pretty steady too. The boy in the red vest had his back to the exit, wasn't even watching.

Joe took advantage of a pause in the outflow and slipped into the property. He was in a stretch of woods maybe twenty feet across. Big trees, mostly pines, no undergrowth to speak of. Somebody put time into keeping it clear. A car went past him. The driver wore a red vest, like the kid on the street. If he saw Joe, he paid no attention—in a hurry to go wherever.

Joe made his way deeper into the property. Trees, a big lawn, flowers, a big white house. Too big. Showy. What rich people liked, he guessed. Not something he had ever wanted. Some people would say, "Good thing you don't, Joe."

And they'd be right.

He stayed in the trees until he came alongside the house. When he could see the front porch, he got a shock. There she was, the pretty lady, greeting the people who were getting out of cars, talking to everybody who came in. Maybe she lived there. Or maybe she was another person hired for the party, hired to smile and look pretty.

Joe stayed put for a while, watching and wondering, hoping this new stakeout would help him figure things out. Then he heard music coming from somewhere and was reminded to wonder, where was Cubby?

It seemed likely the lady would be on the porch as long as people were coming in, and the line of cars was still long, so Joe made his way toward the back of the house, staying in the trees. Yep, that's where the party was happening. Tents, white folding chairs, people. Food, drinks, a trio playing an electric piano, guitar, stand-up bass. Maybe he could just mingle, talk to somebody. But his khakis and plaid shirt wouldn't blend in with the dark suits and fancy dresses.

Joe hadn't spent a lot of time crouching behind shrubs and trees, maybe none before that very day. He found a stump he could sit on while he watched, and it wasn't too bad. Hard on the rear end, but so was the van seat after eight or ten hours of driving. The party crowd filtered across his gaze until he spotted Cubby. Drink in one hand, shaking hands with the other. Making chit-chat like he'd been doing it all his life. Head back, laughing. Jeez. The poor pretty lady stuck out front while this guy had a good time.

The music stopped and people began to sit in the white chairs. A man stepped up to a microphone and started talking.

Five minutes later, Joe heard pop, pop, pop and an explosion. It came from the back property line, off to his left. Some little building he hadn't noticed before—a fireball now.

Joe whipped his head side-to-side, looking at the fireball, looking back at the party. The speechmaker stopped talking or moving, the way a movie stops, freeze-frame. The people in the chairs got up and turned to look toward the explosion.

A spark drifted past Joe, landed in the pine straw mulch, sizzled a second and died. Another one. But they weren't coming from the direction of the fire eating up the little building. Should he move? Run? But no place looked safer than where he was. Then he saw it—the big house on fire, flames pouring out of an upstairs window, rising up over the roof.

Somebody had the microphone, was yelling into it. "Stay calm, don't run, go through the house and out the front."

And Joe was on the move. He got to the man with the mic and grabbed it away from him. "Don't go in, don't go in. The house is on fire, the house is on fire."

And then people really lost their minds.

43

Maureen and Dave took his truck because it had a scanner. By the time they got to the scene in a fancy neighborhood, the street was already blocked off. They knew from the scanner, three stations were responding, cops and emergency medical aid too.

"You have your ID on you?" Dave asked her.

She pulled it out of her shoulder bag. "Let's see if we can get close."

They parked and made their way to the barriers.

"I know this guy," Maureen said when she saw the cop who guarded it.

"Sweet-talk us in," Dave said. And she did.

Once inside the gate and up the driveway, they followed a gravel track that wound around the right side of the house. All the action was at the back. They skirted the pumper trucks, hoses, and ladder crews and found a place where they could see what was going on and be out of the way.

The big white house had an impressive flow of fire out of an upstairs window. Maureen didn't see many actual fires, only the aftermath. It would be hard to contain a fire in an occupied dwelling, full of stuff, all combustible. The best the firefighters could do was limit the flames and ruin what didn't burn with water.

"Damn," Dave said. "I hope to heck nobody's inside. This place could crash in no time."

Men running across the lawn away from the house drew Maureen's eye. A much smaller building had already crumbled to cinders. Firefighters had their hoses trained on the mulched flower beds around it.

"Two sites involved," Maureen said. "How did that happen?"

"Yeah. It's too far for a spark from one to start the other."

"There must have been a party going on." She looked at the chairs tossed all over the place, a long table under a tent, still loaded with food. A portable bar under another tent. "I wonder what happened to all the civilians."

And then she saw him. Joe. He'd already seen her and was bearing down. "Maureen, thank God you're here. It was him, Maureen. Cubby. I saw him."

44

Maureen had been sure she'd seen the last of Joe Corcoran. Her evening with Dave Shepard took care of any last doubts, Joe being out of her life was a good thing. But here he was, bareheaded for a change, panting, his shirttail half out, running straight at her like a crazy man.

"Hey, buddy," Dave said. "Good to see you again. Nothing like a fire scene, huh?"

Joe gave him a blank look like he couldn't quite place Dave, then grinned. "Chief, I told you about this guy. Remember?"

"The one you called a firebug?"

"Wait," Maureen said. "When did you two—?" She stopped herself. While she was picking through the burned-out bath house at the park, the two men had talked. She'd asked if Dave knew Quinn Tatum. But Joe would have said Cubby. And firebug.

"That's the one," Joe said. "He was here tonight. And the lady."

Dave looked at Maureen. "That's a serious coincidence."

Her heart rate was up, way up. She knew Dave's was too.

"No coincidence," Joe said. "I'm telling you, he started these fires."

The three of them were yelling now. Had to yell to be heard over the layers of sound— flames sucking, wood cracking, water roaring like Niagara, men shouting orders and cautions.

"We need to get farther back," Maureen said. "We can't hear each other." Besides, if somebody official saw them, they'd be due a reaming out. Could be the end of Dave's ambitions for a job in Raleigh. They had let their excitement about a big fire overrule good judgment.

Dave took her elbow and tilted his head back the way they'd come. Reality must have kicked in for him too.

They threaded through the woods at the edge of the lot until they got to the front gate and out onto the street. Crowds had gathered at the barricades that closed off the block. The single cop Maureen had known and talked to had been joined by three more.

"You may have to sweet-talk us out like you sweet-talked us in," Dave said.

A different cop challenged them when they got to the barricade. "Where'd you come from?"

"Sorry, officer," Maureen said. "We got lost in the confusion."

"Everybody who was on the scene is supposed to be at the church a block over, giving statements."

"Thanks," Dave said. "We'll go there now. My truck's just over there."

Maureen, Dave, and Joe had to move against the crowd to get to the truck. The streetlights in this neighborhood were genteel, soft—a reminder it was a low-crime area. The three of them huddled in a pool of light.

"All right, Joe," Maureen said. "Tell us what you saw."

He started with what he'd seen the night before when he got back to the hotel from her house. Maureen glanced at Dave. Did he catch that Joe had been to her house? She'd explain later.

Joe went on to tell how Cubby acted all suspicious, coming and going from the Highway Home, and then how he, Joe, followed the Caddy to the party and snuck in. He saw the pretty lady at the front door while Cubby was around back, hobnobbing. Then the little house blew up, and while everybody else was looking that way, it was Joe himself who first saw the flames coming out of the upstairs window. He was the one who grabbed the microphone and hollered for everybody to move away from the house.

"How many people were at this party?" Dave asked.

"A hundred at least. Plus the waiters and cooks and all. People were crying, hugging, acting like they would die any second, but jeez, they weren't in any real danger, you know? They just needed to settle down and walk away. Now the man who owns the place, he was running around cussing and yelling. And a woman—I think it was his wife—it seemed like she couldn't move, but she could sure cry and scream. When the cops got there, they got everybody lined up, marched them out."

"Why didn't you go with the rest of them?" Maureen asked.

"I saw Cubby slink off toward the back of the yard and meant to follow him, but then I remembered about the lady. I hadn't seen her once the fire got going. She might have been inside, could have been trapped. I went around front to where she'd been, and I saw her walking off down the driveway like she didn't have a care in the world."

"Sounds like you need to tell the police all of this," Dave said.

"Wait," Maureen said. "Let's think about it."

The men gave her that look, that we're-listening-little-lady look she was so used to. And knew how to handle.

"Joe, you don't know it, but J.J. Ralston had his eye on you for the Highway Home fire."

"Me?" Joe took a step toward her. Dave took a step toward him.

"Listen to me," Maureen said. "In every arson situation, the first person to rule out is the person who called the fire in. Dave will tell you. It's a reflex."

Joe looked down, as if he'd never seen his shoes before. "You don't think I should tell them?"

"You do what you have to do," she said. "Just know, they're going to hear it their own way. I don't want you to get in trouble." She glanced at Dave. He was studying her the way Joe studied his shoelaces. A vertical crease formed in the middle of his forehead.

"But, Maureen, you know what I know," Joe said. "You've been agreeing with me all along."

True, the idea of a firebug had intrigued her. That's why she'd gone to Littleboro to see the fire chief who turned out to be Dave.

She put a hand on Joe's arm. "The first time I talked to you, you said we're alike because we don't have to have evidence to know something's true. We're not like the cops and firemen that way. Remember?" She waited until he nodded. "But in their world, evidence is everything. You think it's more than a coincidence that Cubby was at both fires. But they'll only have your word for that. They know for a fact, you were at both fires."

"She's right," Dave said. "She's trying to help you out here."

Joe's chin came up and he looked her in the eyes. "Do you think I did it?"

The answer turned out to be easy. "No, I don't."

"OK then, what do you think I should do?"

"What do you want to do?" Maureen said.

"Go to the flipping church and lay it all out."

Maureen glanced at Dave and got a half-smile. "OK," she said. "I'll back you up as best I can."

"My camper van's on a street between here and there," Joe said. "I need to pick it up before it gets a ticket or something."

"We'll drive you," Dave said.

Maureen sat between the two men. Her thigh touched Dave's when he took a corner. Joe leaned hard away from her, like his feelings were still hurt. They found the camper van, and Joe told Dave how to get to the church before he got out of the truck.

"See you there," Dave said. Joe grunted and walked off.

Maureen scooted across the seat, but not all the way over. It was nice, being close to Dave, even though she wondered if he was wishing he'd called it quits after one beer and some wings, headed home to Littleboro a couple of hours earlier.

Joe started the van and made a U-turn. Dave followed.

"Are you ready to tell the investigators you don't think Joe had anything to do with the fires?" Dave asked.

"I said I'd back him up," she said. "What's the worst that can happen?"

The worst was, she'd be vouching for a man in spite of the fact that he looked suspicious to authorities. She'd worked hard to earn trust. If there were no more late-night phone calls to investigate fires in Raleigh, it would hit her income. It would hit her pride worse. But not enough that she could leave Joe to swing in the wind.

Joe led them to a parking lot behind a two-story brick building. A sign read First Baptist Church Fellowship Hall.

"Five police cars," Dave said. "And an ambulance."

"And TV vans." Maureen saw two with local station logos on the doors. They were dark.

Joe drove to a far corner to park. Dave stopped nearer the building. He and Maureen got out and headed for the entrance. Two uniformed officers stood just inside the double doors.

"Good evening, sir, ma'am," one of them said. "Only people who were at the scene of the fire are allowed in right now."

"We were there," Maureen said.

"Can I get your names?" He wrote their names on a list and motioned them in. "Have a seat, and somebody will be with you."

The large multipurpose room was crowded with men in suits, most with their jackets off and ties loosened, and women in cocktail dresses and heels. They sat in clusters at haphazardly placed folding tables and chairs. Conversation was at a low fits-and-starts rumble.

EMTs stood by, leaning against the wall with their arms

crossed, ready if somebody needed attention or passed out. Or threw up. Some of the partygoers looked green around the gills.

Three pairs of police officers sat at tables lined up at the far end of the room, each pair talking to one or two witnesses to the fire. It would take a while to go through all the people.

"Hi, Maureen." Someone tapped her shoulder. "What are you doing here?"

"J.J. Hi." Her face got hot. What was she doing there? "Captain J.J. Ralston, this is Dave Shepard. He's chief of the Littleboro Fire Department. We were eating burgers at the Hideaway and heard sirens, so…"

The men shook hands. "So you had to see what was going on," J.J. said.

"Your trucks rolled right by us," Dave said. "How could we resist?"

"Uh-huh," J.J. said. "Just a Friday night out on the town. Were you at the scene?"

"Things were getting under control by the time we got there," Maureen said.

"Still, you two may be more help than all these civilians."

He wasn't irritated, then. Maureen exhaled. "Weren't you there?"

"I was tied up in a meeting downtown," J.J. said. "Now the police are talking to everybody, and my boss wanted me here. He's a member of this church and got permission for us to use it."

"Any theories about how tonight's fires started?" Dave asked.

"Way too soon to say. Most people seem to agree, the garden shed went up first, and everybody was looking at it when somebody yelled the house was on fire."

Maureen looked at Dave—that somebody was Joe. Where had he gotten to, anyway?

Then he was right there beside her. "Hey, Captain, remember me?"

J.J. squinted. "Yeah. The Highway Home fire. When was that? Two weeks ago? As I recall, you were just passing through."

"Yep, but I'm still here. And guess what..." Joe glanced at Maureen and Dave, then started spilling his theory about Cubby and the pretty lady, picking up where he'd left off with J.J. the first time, going through the park fire, right up through grabbing the microphone tonight.

J.J. listened, and Maureen could see the gears turning in his head. She wished Joe had chickened out. But that wouldn't be Joe.

When Joe wound down, J.J. turned to her. "I read your report on the hotel fire, Maureen."

That was a surprise, like Dave reading her resumé. She was sure that report was dead and buried by the industrial park blaze.

J.J. went on. "I remember the photos with the burned phone book you found, and that paper towel. You pretty well established whoever started the fire had been inside the hotel." He nodded to Joe. "I need for you to tell all this to the police. Let's find the lieutenant."

He put a hand on Joe's arm and directed him toward one of the tables, then he turned back to Maureen. "Can you wait here a minute? I want to talk to you."

After they were gone, Maureen recognized a local TV reporter sitting at a table by himself. He was dressed for work—sports coat, tie, white button-down. He was the reporter she'd seen covering the industrial park fire live as it happened and reporting on it daily ever since.

"Let's find some chairs," Dave said. "This could take a while."

"I want to talk to this guy a minute," she said. "I'll catch up to you."

She approached the reporter. "Hi. I know you. Blaine Autry, Cap City News, right? Is this going to be on the TV?" She hoped she sounded wide-eyed and impressed, but he gave no sign of basking in a fan's recognition. Instead, he clenched his fists and screwed up his mouth, as if he was on the edge of a tantrum.

"It should be the whole news," he said. "I get the biggest break of my career, and the cops say I'm a witness. I can't leave, I can't report, I can't even find a phone and call my producer."

"You were at the fire? Do you know whose house it was?"

"Sure. Senator Wayland's. We were there to cover his big political announcement. I'd just interviewed him on camera not five minutes before the fire started, but he dodged the one question I wanted answered."

"What was that?"

"Had law enforcement kept him up to date on the investigation into the industrial plant fire?"

That was his big question? "Why would they?"

"Because he was a major investor. I'll bet you, whoever blew up the building site set fire to Wayland's house."

It took a moment, then it all came together for Maureen. "You think those fires are connected?"

The man focused on her for the first time. "The senator's investment hasn't been made public before. I was going to break the news tonight and that was big enough, but then his house burns down right in front of me, clearly from arson." He sighed. "It would be a huge story."

She hoped he wasn't going to cry. "Hey, it'll be just as huge tomorrow."

She looked around for Dave. He had found two chairs against the wall. She joined him.

"What was that all about?" Dave asked.

"He's a reporter, and he's all pissed off because he is supposed to be on TV tonight. He's been covering the big fire at the industrial plant, and guess what? The house that burned tonight belongs to one of the investors."

Dave whistled. "The coincidences just don't stop tonight."

"It makes the Highway Home fire look puny. A one-off. Some kind of prank."

They could see Joe across the room, telling his tale one more time with big hand gestures, leaning forward and back as he talked. J.J. stood behind the two police officers who listened and made notes. Maureen watched his face. He gave nothing away.

"You know," Maureen said, "you don't have to wait. I can get Joe to give me a ride. Or call a cab."

"That hurts my feelings, Maureen. I'm not leaving you here. Besides, I'm worried about your buddy too."

After a few minutes, J.J. made his way back to them, and pulled up a chair so he faced the two of them. "Long day," he said, "long night."

"J.J.," Maureen began, "I know Joe's a little much, but I've gotten to know him and—"

"Hang on. You don't need to do that." J.J. put the palms of his hands flat on his knees. "This investigation is going in a different direction. Nothing to do with Joe, nothing to do with the mysterious Cubby."

"Why even interview Joe, then?" Dave asked.

"Because I could tell he'd be a pain in my rear until I got him his moment in the sun," J.J. said.

"See the man over there?" Maureen pointed. "Recognize him from TV? He's a reporter, and he's one of your witnesses. He says the senator is a big investor in the industrial plant project, and he believes whoever set one fire set the other."

"That is not public information." J.J. stood. "I need to find a telephone. Y'all have a good night, and thanks for the heads up."

Joe was on his feet now, too, and coming toward Maureen and Dave. He was grinning.

"We tell him?" Maureen said.

"It's best coming from you."

"I got their attention," Joe said from ten feet away and gave a little fist pump.

"We'll walk you out," Maureen said.

Joe talked while they crossed the parking lot to the camper van. The lieutenant had listened, made notes, said it was good when a citizen came forward, not everybody would.

"Yeah, but..." and Maureen told him what the reporter had said, what J.J. had said, and ended up, "I'm sorry, Joe. The evidence points away from Cubby, at least for tonight."

"You gave it your best shot," Dave said. "And we may never know the truth."

Joe didn't speak right away. He looked past them toward the lighted building they'd just left, and finally said, "Yeah, well. It's what I do, you know?"

He shook Dave's hand and patted Maureen on the shoulder. "Y'all take care." Then he got in the van and drove off.

Maureen wished she and Joe could have left things the way they were the day before at her front door, a friendly goodbye with the promise of postcards from the road.

"You did the right thing," Dave said, "standing up for him." He turned in the direction of his truck. "Ready to go?"

She fell in beside him. "When the time came, I couldn't not. Even though it didn't matter, I guess."

"Can I ask you something? When you came to my office to leave off your card, ask if we'd had any unexplained fires in the county, were you working on an investigation like you said, or just fishing?"

"I was fishing."

"Did Joe have anything to do with it?"

"Nope. It was all my own curiosity. Sorry."

"Why sorry? You turned out to be the person I needed for the Great Littleboro Conflagration of 1976."

She laughed. When Dave opened the door for her, did he put his arm around her first, or did she lean into him? Did he kiss her first, or did she kiss him? Did it matter?

They had to go back to the restaurant to get her car. He followed her home.

45

It was midnight before Joe got back to the Highway Home. One of the security lights, the one nearest where the fire had been, was out. Dang Terry. He needed to watch TV less, tend to business more.

The Caddy was not in its spot. Room 314 was not just dark. It looked like a place where there had never been light. Joe's gut told him, they were gone. Long gone.

All the way from the church to the hotel, Joe had imagined banging on Cubby's door, yelling, "You're in trouble now, buckaroo. The cops are coming for you."

But he knew they weren't coming. They'd listened to him, recorded him even, found the name Quinn Tatum on the guest list the senator had provided. But the longer he'd talked, the more they leaned back in their chairs, crossed their arms, traded side-eyed glances. And Ralston stood behind the cops, looking down at Joe.

Finally, the lieutenant thanked Joe and told him he could go, saying they would talk to the senator, ask what he knew about Mr. Tatum. He said it like he was serious, but Joe knew now, Cubby was off the hook. At least in the eyes of the law.

He backed into his usual spot and cut the engine. Did he want to sleep under that roof one more night, even if he had paid for it? He could slide in, collect his shaving kit, his paperbacks, his box of snack food, whatever else was still in the room. Get ice for the cooler. He could leave twenty dollars—no, three tens—in an envelope for June, Deb, and Linda, drop his key on the desk for Terry to find in the morning.

Then he'd head west, drive as long as he could stay awake, find a place to pull over for the night, and leave Raleigh and everybody in it in the rearview mirror. There would be somebody out there in the vastness of the country who needed him.

46

Lammie lay on her side, snuggled up against Cubby's back. It felt familiar now, as if they'd been like this forever. It was how they would be every night for the rest of their lives.

They'd driven south and stopped at a Holiday Inn in South Carolina. They would turn westward the next day, take a southern route for California. Cubby had carried the footlocker with the money into the room rather than leave it in the car, because she said she wanted to be near it.

She thought about how she'd followed his instructions, made the 911 call, avoided getting caught up in the crowd of panicking people, walked out the front gate, and found him waiting in the car at the end of the block, the motor idling. By the time she slid into the Cadillac and leaned over for a kiss, they heard sirens.

"What took you so long? What did you do?" Cubby

asked, cold, the way he'd been when she first told him she stole money.

She told him, and he was angry, but that was because she put herself in danger. She could have been trapped in a burning house. The garden shed would have been enough. It would have broken up the party, made sure the news reports were about it and not the senator's announcement. Didn't she know he wanted her safe? Didn't she know how much she meant to him?

He'd broken his own vow not to deal with fire anymore, just to make her happy, to get the revenge she deserved. And she'd promised him already, she would never, ever do it again.

Had she promised? She wasn't sure she had—and now he made her say it over and over, no more, never again.

She said it as many times as he wanted, of course she did.

Lammie lay awake in the dark room, happier than she'd ever been, watching the constellation of freckles on his neck glow, sparks that would never die.

June 20, 1981

47

Saturday morning. Maureen rolled over in bed. She heard the radio in the kitchen. Alabama, "Love in the First Degree." And Dave singing along, loud and off-key, mostly to annoy Kimmy, who complained, "Daaaad," drawing the word out as long as she had breath for.

The music changed. "Start Me Up," then switched off. Dave didn't think his little girl should listen to the Stones. Little girl. She was fourteen. Some days going on thirty, some going on six.

But Kimmy was up, at least. That was more than Maureen could say. She rolled over and looked at the clock. Almost nine. Sweet Dave, letting her sleep in while he made breakfast for his kids. Maureen pulled the covers over her head, not to block out the sounds of family, or the scent of coffee. No, that was almost enough to get her up.

Moments like this, she still had to stop and absorb what had happened: Marriage, step-momhood, every-other-weekend parenting, teaching fire investigation courses in the criminal justice program at the community college. A newer, bigger house. And Dave. Especially Dave. How it had happened, she hadn't a clue.

Somebody tapped on the bedroom door. "Maureen?" It was Brian. "Dad says pancakes are ready. Are you awake?"

"Coming. I'll get the next batch."

She went to the bathroom, brushed her teeth, combed her hair, put on a robe, and went to the kitchen. Kimmy and Brian were at the table eating. Kimmy glanced at Maureen and nodded, her mouth too full to speak. Brian, still a cuddler at eleven, jumped up and hugged her around the waist, chewing the whole time.

"Hey, babe," Dave said. "I got two with your name on them. And check the paper."

The newspaper lay on her plate, folded to an article on an inside page. Maureen picked it up. The headline read "Former NC Woman Charged in Arson Cases."

"Nothing like arson on a Saturday morning," Maureen said. She read on, then looked up. Dave was watching her.

"Read it out loud," he said. "I want to hear it again."

"From Jackson, Wyoming. 'Mary Lambert Tatum, formerly of Littleboro, NC, was arrested in her hospital room on Thursday where she was recovering from second-degree burns and smoke inhalation. Tatum was charged with a series of arson fires in US national parks over a period of three years. The fires were confined to visitors' centers and other structures after closing hours when few if any people were near them. Property damage was extensive, but no one was injured.

"'Tatum sustained her injuries when she was unable to escape a building where authorities believe she set a fire.

Tatum's 1974 Cadillac was impounded as evidence. The car, or one like it, had been seen at or near numerous fire scenes over a period of several weeks. Her husband, Quinn Tatum, was questioned at his home in Littleboro. People who know him say he had returned to his hometown last month to bury his aunt and attend to family business. He said through an attorney that his wife was a troubled woman. He would be returning to Wyoming as quickly as possible. The authorities have not ruled out charging him with obstruction for failing to report her previous activities to law enforcement.'"

Maureen dropped the paper on top of the pancakes Dave had slid onto her plate, picked it up again. "I don't believe it. After all this time."

"Who are these people?" Kimmy asked. "Do you know them?"

The telephone rang.

"I'll get it." Brian jumped up. "Hello. Hey, Joe. Yeah, they're both here. Which one do you want to talk to? OK." He stretched the long cord from the wall-mounted phone to Maureen.

"You've seen the paper, I guess," she said into the receiver.

Joe Corcoran was so loud, Maureen had to hold the phone away from her ear. "Hell yeah I saw it. Didn't I say? Five years ago, didn't I say it was him?"

"Yeah, Joe," Dave yelled, "you told us. But it's the lady they've arrested."

"We're coming over," Joe yelled back, and the line went dead.

Maureen got up to put the receiver in the cradle. "We" meant Joe and June, the woman who had worked at the

Highway Home when he stayed there and was now the manager.

"Are you going to eat those, Maureen?" Brian aimed a fork at Maureen's plate.

"Yes, she is," Dave said. "I'll cook more."

"If Joe's coming over, I'm going to Becky's." Kimmy got bored with what she called Joe's blah-blah. She put her plate in the sink and tolerated Dave kissing the side of her head.

"So, if I call in a little while, Becky's mom will confirm you're there?" he said.

"Maybe." She bolted.

"Can I go to Becky's too?" Maureen said. "Remind me why it seemed like a good idea to rent my house to Joe when he finally decided to get off the road."

Joe had kept his promise to send postcards to Maureen, and, it turned out, to June at the Highway Home Hotel as well. After a couple of years back on the road, he turned up in Raleigh again, saying it was time to settle down.

"What's going on, anyway?" Brian said.

Dave answered. "Five years ago, about the time I met Maureen, there were a few fires around here. Could have been a firebug at work. Joe was still living in his van and traveling around the country, but he happened to be in town at the time, and he thought the husband of the woman they've arrested set those fires. Nobody could prove it, though." Dave dropped two more pancakes in front of his son.

"OK." Brian smeared butter and poured syrup over his plate. "What time's practice today?"

"Didn't we agree, you will keep up with your own schedule from now on?" Maureen said.

"I know. It's at eleven." Brian's grin always got to her, a lot like his father's. "I'm just testing you."

She reached out to pinch his arm. "Wise guy."

The back door opened, and Joe appeared, June behind him, laughing and shaking her head.

Joe yanked off his red ball cap. "They'll believe me now, right?"

ACKNOWLEDGMENTS

First, I want to acknowledge and thank Kelly Prelipp Lojk, copy editor and book designer extraordinaire. And a lovely friend, to boot.

Then, the writers who have at different stages of this book's journey from my imagination to the reader's hands given me sharp-witted, sharp-eyed, thoughtful, and always supportive advice: Joyce Allen, Paula Blackwell, Kim Church, Rebecca Duncan, Ashley Harris, Ruth Moose, and Pat Walker. Ruth gets an extra serving of gratitude for allowing Lammie and Cubby to occupy the town she created, Littleboro, North Carolina. Three other early readers, Steve Esthimer, Judith Gaines, and Patti Meredith, were excellent critics. The book readers hold is better thanks to them.

Two of my writing teachers, Max Steele and Barbara Lorie, are no longer with us, but energy is eternal, and their energy is always with me.

Families have a way of shrinking over time and then expanding again in wonderful ways. My Gaskin and Esthimer families have both grown since I last thanked them for their support. A new generation is beautiful, growing, and thriving. They are my source of optimism.

I am fortunate to have dear friends—many going back more decades than we like to count. A yoga teacher taught me to feel the columns of air that support my extended hands. It's the same kind of invisible but always there support I feel from those friends. You know who are. Thank you.

Table Rock Writers Workshop under the leadership of Georgann Eubanks and Donna Campbell is home to many writers. I'm so glad to be one of them. See you on the mountain, y'all!

I dedicated the book to my husband, Steve Esthimer. He makes me laugh (the secret to a long marriage, I do believe) and makes everything better. He is also an eagle-eyed proofreader. Who could ask for more?

NORA GASKIN is a lifelong resident of North Carolina's Durham-Chapel Hill area. She has a bachelor's degree in English with honors in creative writing from UNC, and a masters in English from the University of Washington in Seattle.

She spent more than twenty-four years as a stockbroker and financial advisor with a major investment firm, working in the Durham office. She retired in 2005 to focus on writing.

Her first published novel, *Until Proven: A Mystery in 2 Parts*, appeared in 2012. While the book is entirely fiction, the seed for it was a real murder that happened in Chapel Hill on Christmas Eve, 1963. In 2013, Nora published a nonfiction book about that Christmas Eve murder, *Time of Death*, to further explore the questions it raised. Her second novel, *The Worst Thing*, appeared in May 2018.

Her small, non-traditional publishing company, Lystra Books, launched in 2013. It has published more than forty books as of 2025, with more on the horizon.

She lives and writes in Chatham County, inspired by her native landscape, her husband, and dogs. Her favorite expression is "y'all means all." Her favorite word is *gratitude*.

www.ingramcontent.com/pod-product-compliance
Lightning Source LLC
LaVergne TN
LVHW041911070526
838199LV00051BA/2576